Slave to Pleasure

BRIDES OF CARALON

LACEY ALEXANDER

The Brides of Caralon series is dedicated to Leonie Daniels, who first encouraged me to try my hand at erotica, and to Anya Bast, who gave me a helpful tip or two along the way.

CHAPTER ONE

3591 AD

A S A WARM touch came on her shoulder, Laela turned to look into her mother's eyes.

"It is time, Daughter. You must take your place before your father's throne."

Laela drew in a deep breath. This was it—the moment she'd awaited her whole life. Her father, ruler of Caralon, was ready to announce the name of her bridegroom.

Her mother, Jalal, always so strong and regal, offered a reassuring smile. "Don't be afraid. You see how well your sisters' marriages have worked out."

Laela nodded. She *wasn't* afraid—she was excited. After all, both her older sisters had been given in marriage to virile, rugged men who seemingly made them happy in every way. Now she was about to get a virile, rugged man of her own. The spot between her thighs clenched at the thought and her nipples tightened beneath the silk that shrouded them. Thank Ares she had finally reached bride's age and would now learn all the secrets of marriage that were kept from royal girls. "I'm ready, mother."

As Jalal led Laela toward her father's throne, set upon a platform at one end of the great hall, the crowd around them grew quiet, understanding the important moment was at hand. Enrick, her father, had called weeks ago for the grand feast they'd all just eaten, inviting visitors from far and wide, but only tonight had he announced that he'd decided to whom he would give Laela's hand in marriage—not to mention her virginity, her bride price.

Having both her sisters in attendance for such a momentous occasion comforted her. A quick glance at Maven and her warrior husband Dane, then to Teesia and her dark-haired Ralen, reminded her once more that she would soon know the same joys as they. Her whole body tingled at the realization that after this night, her life would change forever—she would finally be a woman, a wife, a *lover*. Oh, how she wanted a man—a man to hold her, a man to love her, a man she could explore and touch and learn about. A man who would ease the aching of that tender, hungry spot that yearned for release—a man who would *give* her the release she'd found herself, with her hand, late at night in the privacy of her bedchamber.

Her father's eyes smiled on her as she neared, and it struck her how much power he held—perched high on his throne made of valuable antique metals from the Before Times. He'd brought peace to a region that had never known it before, and he'd united that region under his rule. He was the most revered man in the domain, and now he was delivering her into her future.

"Laela, my youngest daughter," he began, his deep voice booming over the vast hall, "in three days, you will be given to your husband-to-be—Ogran of the Mountains."

As the crowd gasped, Laela felt lightheaded and actually stumbled backward. She caught herself and remained upright as she tried to process what her father had just said. *Ogran of the Mountains?* No! How could it be?

She swallowed nervously, her heart thudding like a drum in her chest, her legs gone weak, then managed to ask the question she knew she must. "Father, the only Ogran I know of is…" Old. Terribly old. *Unthinkably* old. "Perhaps…Ogran has a *son*, or a *grandson*, of the same name?" she asked, trying to understand.

Her father's lips pursed and she could have sworn the wrinkles at his eyes slashed a bit deeper. He looked almost sad as he replied, yet his voice came strong and sure. "No, my daughter, Ogran has no son. He is the man you have met here in our fortress."

She remembered his visits when she was a very little girl—he'd been an old man even then. Bile roiled in her stomach, any fluttering she'd been experiencing between her thighs now a thing of the past. "But Father…" She was at a loss for words and knew she need not even speak them—her complaint was clear enough without voicing it. *How could you do this to me? How could you?*

Enrick spoke softly, kindly. "He wishes a wife, children."

"And in return?" she asked, her voice growing cold.

"His forces will guard our western borders from encroachers through the mountain passes."

She nodded shortly, fully understanding now. Her father had given her sisters in marriage to men who lived on the borders as well, men who could protect Caralon from enemies trying to invade—but he'd also chosen men with whom he'd known they would ultimately be well matched. In Laela's case, he'd apparently sold her for border protection without a care for her happiness. She let her accusing gaze burn into him without concern for the roomful of people around them.

"Come closer, Daughter," Enrick bade. He bent down to speak, low enough that only she could hear. "He will die, Laela. And then his estate will be yours. It is a good arrangement."

"For *you*," she snapped, not replying in quite so discreet a tone.

"For you, too. Once he passes, you will be free to do whatever you wish, and you will be wealthy, as well."

Her back went rigid. "So you're banishing me to a place so remote it doesn't even have a real name in order that I might be wife to a man who could easily be my grandfather, and you think having only to live this way for five or ten years until he dies is a *good arrangement*?" She'd never spoken to her father so shrilly and she'd not have been surprised had he struck her down with the back of his hand.

But instead, his sad look remained in place. "Laela, it is not ideal, I admit. But the western borders are being threatened. Dane has kept the Virgs to the north contained, but there are others—tribal people—coming together beyond our western rim, and they could intend our domain great harm. There has also been talk of the Virgs circling down to invade through the mountains, as well. Ogran was…the only choice."

"I am a pawn," she returned softly.

"Caralon must be kept safe, this you know."

She snorted in disdain and turned to go, yet stopped to look back at her father one last time. "I never thought you'd forsake me," she spat, then walked back down the path she'd come, eyes on the smooth stone floor before her, unwilling to glance up at the astonished onlookers. Her skin crawled with disgust over her own fate.

I must get out of this room, now. I must be alone where I can think and somehow try to figure out how I'm going to survive this.

But already she knew that thinking wasn't going to help.

Her life was about to become a nightmare.

LAELA LAY ON her bed, hugging her black cat, Midnight, to her breasts. She knew everyone at the fortress thought it a bit odd that she'd taken such a liking to the stable cat, even bringing it indoors and giving it a name—

people didn't form such personal attachments to that sort of animal—but ever since her sisters had married and left home, leaving her virtually alone in the world, she'd needed a friend, and that friend had become Midnight. "At least I'll have *you* with me," she said, looking into the cat's green eyes, which reminded her of the rare round, green marbles she'd seen from the Before Times. "Even if we *are* being banished to 'the mountains'." She rolled her eyes at the very notion. Just like her sister Teesia, she loved the ocean, and she found it difficult to imagine life without it nearby.

Then again, she was having a hard time imagining *any* part of the new life she'd just been sentenced to. Glancing in the general direction of the great hall, she sneered her anger at her father. She'd always felt like the odd-one-out in her family, and this only proved she was right. Maven was her father's eldest and favorite, her looks echoing his blonde hair and fair complexion, while Teesia mirrored their mother more—in both appearance and temperament, with long dark locks and an eager determination to get what she wanted at all costs. Laela, with her plain brown hair and a face she'd always thought of as pretty but not *striking*, was not particularly much like her mother *or* her father—and she was no one's particular favorite.

Yet, even so, she was loved within her family and she'd never have believed her father would simply abandon her this way! Clearly, he didn't value her as much as his other two daughters. Clearly, he saw her life as something disposable.

Just then, both Maven and Teesia came rushing in to the bedchamber, their silk dresses flowing around their curves like ocean waves. With their long hair falling about their shoulders like decadent waterfalls—while Laela's remained in the braid that signified her royal virginity—it was one more reminder that they both lived the perfect life she ached for, and now had no chance of ever achieving.

Both sisters' eyes brimmed with horror on her behalf. "Oh Laela," Maven said, hugging her close as she plopped on the fur-covered bed next to her. Midnight screeched and leapt from her arms, dashing under the large wooden wardrobe in the corner.

"You must be strong, Laela," Teesia said. "You must fight your way through this, and before you know it, Ogran will be dead and then you can be like my friend, Bella, flitting from bed to bed with whomever you please." She finished with a smile, as if her words had actually made the situation more palatable.

"It's a bit difficult to think that far ahead at the moment," Laela replied with a scowl.

Even as Maven continued clinging to her, Teesia sat down on her other side and took her hands. "I know, but you must focus on the positive...and, well, that's the only positive I've come up with so far." With that, Teesia's eyes dropped to the stone floor, as if she'd misspoken. "I'm so sorry Father has done this to you."

Laela answered honestly. "I just thought he'd choose

someone for me like Dane or Ralen. Some-one…masculine, handsome. Someone who might please me. I've been waiting so long to be with a man…" She trailed off into a forlorn sigh.

Maven suddenly shot one finger triumphantly into the air. "I have a positive for you to focus on! The Rituals of Passion!"

"Rituals of Passion?" Laela echoed.

"Yes, that's right!" Teesia answered, her expression becoming just as lively. "I did not get to have them—due to Ralen's rather forceful ways, but Maven did, didn't you, Maven?"

Maven nodded. "It's what happens after the marriage ceremony, after the game of Maran tiles. It is sinfully pleasurable, Laela—in a way that need not have to do with your husband, exactly—and once you know such pleasures, you can simply…well, you can concentrate on *them* afterward. Perhaps you can remember them at…unpleasant times. You can close your eyes and travel back to the Rituals of Passion whenever you have need to."

Teesia spoke up then. "But remember, do not try to play an especially good game of Maran tiles—right, Maven?"

"Yes, that's right! Play poorly and you will get more and more pleasure for it. Your pussy will hum like it never has before and your breasts will ache most delightfully, and then you will be introduced to the cock—"

"Pussy? Cock?" Laela repeated, perplexed.

Teesia rolled her eyes at Maven. "Stop. You're confusing her with words she doesn't yet know."

Her sisters were talking so fast that Laela *indeed* felt thoroughly befuddled looking back and forth between them. "I don't understand. What *are* these Rituals of Passion exactly? What will happen to me when—"

At that moment, the thick wooden door to her room burst open and all three sisters went instantly still. It was unheard of to tell a royal bride what she could expect on her wedding night, especially concerning the Maran tiles.

Fortunately, it was only their mother, allowing them all to breathe a collective sigh of relief. Jalal's dark hair shone in dramatic contrast against her usual sky blue silk as her eyes locked on Laela. "It is time for your Orientation, Daughter."

The girls began to exchange looks of doubt and fear and dread. How could they be separated *now*? Laela had so much more to learn from her sisters before she was subjected to marrying Ogran of the Mountains. It was Maven who finally spoke. "Mother, could we just have a few more minutes with Laela? She is frightened and she needs our counsel."

Jalal let out a regretful sigh as she shook her head. "I'm sorry, but your Orienter is here and it's time to begin."

"Mother," Laela beseeched her, pushing to her feet, "you cannot possibly be behind Father's decision." Yes, Jalal had backed Enrick when he'd matched Maven with

"Dane the Dreadful," and that had turned out to be for the best—but this was altogether different.

Jalal released another long breath. "I will admit I'm troubled by your father's decision, Laela. But you know he is not a man who changes his mind, and if he has chosen this path for you, it will stand."

Obviously seeing the hurt in Laela's eyes, Jalal moved toward her, taking her youngest girl's hands. "I'm truly sorry, Daughter. I would not have wished this for you." She drew back to look at her, eyes filled with faith and resolve. "But you are stronger than you know. You will survive this. And your life will ultimately be good. I feel it in my heart."

Within a too-short moment, Laela had hugged her sisters and mother goodbye, all of them shedding a few tears as she tried to accept her horrible fate. Over and again, the question pummeled her—*How can this be? How can my father expect me to endure such a marriage?*

The despairing thoughts were interrupted when her private teacher for the past several years, Aris, entered the room. Aris' brown hair was darker than Laela's chestnut-colored locks, and fell straighter and more fine, nearly to her waist. Laela had always thought her a pretty woman, but quiet and prim—not the norm for a single woman in Caralon where, so long as you were not of royalty, you could live whatever lifestyle you pleased, having a different man in your bed every night if you chose. She'd never seen Aris with *any* man and was surprised the young teacher had been selected to play this particular role in Laela's life. "You are to be my Orienter, Aris?"

Aris smiled thinly, looking slightly uncomfortable. "I, too, was shocked when your mother asked me, but she reminded me that you and I have always gotten on well and that this is key for your Orientation."

"True enough." But even so, it seemed this might be awkward. Up to now, Laela had been bubbling with excitement at the prospect of learning from her Orienter about what happened between a man and a woman—the sensations in her breasts and between her thighs, the way she rubbed herself there sometimes and reached the most spectacular summit of pleasure. Now, however, such enthusiasm was difficult to fathom.

"Shall we begin?" Aris asked.

Laela nodded, though her mind still swam with worries. How could she embrace this particular royal marriage ritual given the man she was expected to marry?

"Very well then," Aris said, and stepped back out into the corridor to start carrying in charts and lists and drawings similar to those Laela was familiar with from their lessons in language and geography.

"Take a seat on the bed, Laela," her teacher instructed as she took up her pointer—a long, smooth stick carved from cherry wood that she always used during lessons—and aimed it toward the first word in a list of many. Aris had never been one to waste a moment of time in class, and this was no exception, as she dove right into her lesson.

"Sex," she said. "Sex is the common term for what

happens between a man and woman." She drew the pointer slightly down to the next word. "This is also called fucking. To fuck is to have sex." Again, the pointer moved lower. "Cunt is one name for your—"

"Wait," Laela injected. "Stop."

Aris looked up, clearly taken aback at having the lesson interrupted. "What is it?"

Laela swallowed. She knew she must somehow get past this, but how? "Aris, my father has condemned me to marriage with…an old man. The idea of being physical with him in any way makes me feel ill." As if echoing her words, her stomach churned at the thought.

As Aris came to join her on the bed, her eyes softened—Laela recognized the look as the same one of sympathy her mother and sisters had imparted. Aris stayed silent for a moment, then said, "Perhaps you will take a lover outside of marriage if you so dare. Some women in arranged marriages do."

That thought filled Laela with simultaneous hope and fear.

"And if not, when Ogran dies, you can take *many* lovers. You will be free, and still young and beautiful enough to indulge in any man you desire."

"That's what everyone says. But in the meantime, how am I to learn the ways of the marriage bed when my stomach shrivels with every thought of the man I am to wed?"

Aris appeared deep in thought for a moment, until she finally looked up at Laela with a speculative smile.

"Think of someone else. During our lessons. And afterward, whenever you need to."

"Someone else? Who?"

Aris' green eyes widened at the prospect. "Is there some handsome man you've seen or know who you might wish to be close to? Who might make your body tingle with arousal when you are near him?"

Laela turned the question over in her head. The first male to come to mind was Donnell, of her father's fortress, who had once been smitten with Maven. Sometimes when Donnell looked at her, the ever-so-sensitive region between her thighs burned and ached to know him better. And there was also the dark blond man in the village. Even darker stubble generally covered his chin, his angular jawline was strong and slightly forbidding, and since the first time Laela had noticed him a year or two ago she couldn't help looking for him whenever they ventured into town. Unlike most villagers of Myrtell, he never came to fortress events, but she'd seen him on shopping excursions and the walks she and her maid sometime took on the beach that passed by the liveliest part of the settlement. Donnell was young and handsome enough, but the slightly dangerous air of the blond stranger drew her thoughts to him in a more forceful way. "I…think I have someone in mind," she told Aris cautiously.

The teacher smiled, then reached to gently squeeze Laela's knee through her pale yellow silken gown. "Good. Now you need only concentrate on *him* as we continue and all will be well."

From there, Aris proceeded with the lesson, teaching Laela terms she'd never heard before—or at least not before her conversation with her sisters a little while earlier—all of which she committed to memory. The teacher used drawings and diagrams to explain exactly what sex was—and Laela couldn't help being astounded at the concept of each man having such a shaft extend from his body as Aris' drawings showed. Not to mention the fact that men *entered* this appendage into the opening between a woman's legs! She couldn't imagine anything more intimate and felt a little stunned to realize how many people were engaging in such acts all the time, all around her, yet keeping it from her virgin eyes.

Of course, her thoughts flitted back to wrinkled old Ogran, but she quickly banished thoughts of him for the blond man from Myrtell who was quickly becoming her fantasy lover, the man who touched her breasts and pussy in the way Aris described, who slid his cock into her wet cunt, which grew wetter still as she envisioned it, as she nearly *felt* him next to her. As the lesson proceeded, Laela suspected that this *sex* she was learning about was even more intense and pleasurable than she'd imagined.

An hour later, when Laela's head was filled with visions of different sexual positions and all the new words that described them, Aris said, "Now, although it may be awkward, you must disrobe and we will remove your hair."

Laela reached up to the back of her head, grasping

her braid protectively. "My hair?"

Aris laughed. "Your body hair, Laela. We will be removing it from the waist down," she explained, then walked to the door and admitted several young men bearing a wooden tub and ewers of water to fill it. One of them was Donnell, whose smile felt purely sexual. Then again, perhaps that was only in her mind, given all she'd just learned. And now she was forced to realize the strapping young men had apparently been waiting outside all this time, possibly hearing their discussion through the crack at the bottom of the door. At the very least, they knew what lessons took place here.

At last, one of the boys placed an expensive glass jar into Aris' hand—filled with blue paste. "The rich use this to remove hair from the legs and pussy," she said, the boys not quite yet gone from the room.

Her face reddened slightly and her cunt twitched as the door finally closed behind them. "But…why?"

Aris smiled. "Many men prefer smooth skin in these areas. It's considered a great luxury."

Laela nodded uncertainly, then followed Aris' instructions to take off her gown and step into the small round tub, trying not to feel shy about her nudity. She listened as Aris spoke more, about men and their preferences—they even liked for women to take their cocks in their mouths!—and she watched as Aris smoothed the blue ointment over her calves and thighs, then her cunt. That particular area felt unusually sensitive to the touch as Aris generously applied the paste, and Laela was almost sorry when the application was done.

Minutes later, Aris used a wet cloth to wash the blue paste away. When her hair disappeared, Laela had never felt smoother—or more on display. The notion made her whole body tingle strangely. It was odd enough to be naked before her teacher, but now she had not even her pussy curls for modesty.

Aris handed her the small viewing glass from her dresser. "Look," she said, "and see how pretty your cunt is now."

Laela peered carefully into the jagged bits of assembled antique glass, surprised at the appearance of her denuded mound and studying in particular the way bits of pink flesh protruded from the slit there. She found it at once arousing and disquieting. "Is this normal? For this flesh to jut out?"

Aris' soft laughter caught her off guard. "Yes, Laela," she said kindly. "But your question tells me that perhaps it is time to get you better acquainted with that part of yourself."

Laela tilted her head, curious. "How?"

Aris took her hand and led her from the tub, reaching for a drying cloth which she used to blot the wetness from Laela's legs. "Come," she said, "sit before me on the rug."

Together, the two young women sat down on the sizable brown fur rug that covered the stone floor at the foot of Laela's bed. To Laela's surprise, Aris swiftly lifted her own thin white leather skirt—all the way to her waist!

Laela gasped, then noticed how her reaction had pinkened Aris' cheeks. "Don't be shocked, Laela—this is uncommon for me, too. But it is the only way I know to teach you."

With that, the teacher spread her legs wide and Laela couldn't help studying her cunt. It still bore hair—wavy tufts of pale brown—and it seemed to open of its own accord, revealing more of the pink folds Laela had seen hints of on herself in the viewing glass. The sight turned her shockingly warm.

To continue the lesson, Aris took up her pointer once more, directing the tip toward the top of her parted pussy. "This is the clit, which we discussed earlier."

"The primary source of pleasure," Laela replied studiously, her eyes riveted on the teacher's tiny glistening knob of pink.

Aris nodded, then moved the pointer lower, using her free hand to spread her flesh even more deeply until Laela saw a small opening, like a tiny cave to nowhere. Only she suspected it definitely led *somewhere*. "This is where the cock enters," Aris explained.

Laela sighed her response, aware that her whole body was rippling with an odd anticipation—an excitement— she'd never expected to experience at her Orientation.

"Are you thinking of your special man's cock going into you?" Aris asked with an uncharacteristically sly smile.

Actually, she had *not* been thinking of that, too caught up in the lesson itself, but now she envisioned her blond fantasy lover sliding into her, feeling pleasurably hard as Aris had described. Or she was *trying* to envision it, anyway. "I am, but…"

"Yes?"

"Up to now, I have always just…"

Aris leaned forward slightly. "You have always just what?"

Laela swallowed back her nervousness—this was no time for that. "I have always just rubbed my clit. I have never been quite so aware of that lower part," she said, pointing to Aris' moist, open cunt. "So even though I want to imagine the cock going into me, it's difficult. For one thing, it's hard to envision something so sizable going into such a small place. And for another…well, I can't quite imagine *anything* going in there." Heat climbed her cheeks by the time she finished speaking— she felt so ignorant. Such was the price of being a royal daughter, kept so purposely unaware of sex and everything related to it.

But when she gathered the courage to lift her gaze to Aris, the teacher's eyes sparkled with kindness. "I can understand how shocking some of this must be to you, Laela. So perhaps," she said, "we should start to Orient you a bit *physically* here, as well."

Laela drew in her breath. "How?"

"Spread your legs for me, Laela. Very wide."

Slowly, Laela did as Aris instructed, parting her

thighs as broadly as she could across the fur rug.

Glancing down at Laela's newly opened pussy, Aris moved closer to her, propping up the small viewing glass before it for Laela to see. "Use your fingers to open yourself more for me."

Darting her eyes to Aris just briefly, Laela followed the command. Her every nerve ending seemed to tingle, her body gone tense as she continued to look into the jagged pieces of glass.

Moving the glass slightly to one side, Aris then knelt between Laela's legs and poised the tip of her pointer at Laela's cunt. At this, Laela tensed further, unduly aroused. Her nipples had long ago hardened into stiff buds, but now they felt particularly tight and sensitive as she sat naked and waiting for what would come next.

Biting her lower lip, Aris nudged the pointer at Laela's flesh, seeking entry. "Relax," she said soothingly when Laela went even more rigid.

Laela tried, remembering that she *wanted* to know what it felt like to be entered. *Relax. Relax your body. Especially there.*

A second later, the wooden pointer slid smoothly in, the sensation no less than shocking and exquisite. She let out a gasp of pleasure just before she and Aris exchanged a smile.

"Of course a cock is much thicker," Aris reminded her, "but at least now you know what it is to be entered."

Laela nodded, her whole body aquiver, as Aris began to slide several inches of the pointer in and out of her pussy. "This is what the man does with his cock, how he fucks you."

Laela sighed with happy realization. "So you are fucking me now. In a way."

Aris giggled lightly, watching her task below very closely. "Yes, in a way."

"I want to see better," Laela admitted in a burst of frustration as the smooth wood slid against her inner flesh.

But it was impossible to position the viewing glass properly with the pointer in the way.

Rising up slightly, Aris smiled, her dark eyebrows lifting slightly. "I have a solution. You can watch it move in and out of *me*." With that, she sat back, situating herself at the opposite, slightly thicker end of the wooden dowel, raising her skirt again so that her parted cunt was put back on display. Laela watched as the teacher smoothly slid the pointer into *her* pussy, as well, the two women's legs crossing over each other's to accommodate the length of the small rod.

"Oh my," Laela said, further aroused at the sight, and amazed that she, too, had the same tool inside of *her*.

"Move against it," Aris said softly. "Follow my lead. Thrust as I do."

Laela watched as Aris shifted her hips, moving them to take the thin rod in deeper, then pulling back to release it slightly. Concentrating very hard, she mimicked the move, struggling to find the exact rhythm, until Aris said, "Yes, that's right. That's right."

Soon, Aris reached down to rub her clit as she fucked the pointer. Her eyelids began to droop heavily and her mouth fell open in a soft moan. Laela watched raptly, caught up in witnessing Aris' obvious pleasure.

"Rub yourself, too," Aris said, her voice coming lower.

"Hmm?" Laela was utterly lost in watching her teacher, as well as the sensation of the pointer moving in and out of her own little hole.

"Rub your clit. Make yourself come." *Coming.* One of the words she'd learned a whole new meaning for during the early parts of their lesson. "You will sleep much easier tonight if you come first, I promise you."

It seemed a private sort of thing, but if Aris didn't mind coming in front of *her*, then Laela decided she need not be so shy. Pulling her gaze from Aris' pussy just long enough to focus on her own, she lowered her first two fingers there, noticing that it felt a bit different with no hair.

And oh, the pleasure! She had not realized how much in need of her own touch she was until the hot delight shot through her. It was motivation enough to make her forget her timidity and proceed to thoroughly press and rub and squeeze the engorged nub of pink flesh Aris had taught her about.

When Aris began to fill the air with deeper sighs and more passionate moans, Laela no longer held hers back either. She continued to watch Aris pleasuring herself, noting how wet and swollen her cunt now appeared, and she thought once more of the handsome man from the village, and imagined *her* hand was *his*, imagined—insanely perhaps—*both* of his hands, one on her clit, the other on Aris', rubbing, rubbing, so slickly into their drenched flesh, pleasuring them both, rubbing harder and harder…and then she exploded.

Oh Ares! The hot pulses of delight shot through her more intensely than anything she'd ever felt alone in her bedchamber. *Orgasm.* That was the word she'd learned for that hot, hard peak of pleasure that took her over now, and which—if she wasn't mistaken—was taking Aris over, too. Both cried out in repletion, again and again, until finally the heat faded and the room went quiet once more.

As Aris glanced down, removing the pointer from herself, then easing it gently from Laela's pussy, as well, she looked slightly sheepish. "I did not intend…" she began softly, "for things to become so…well, I had not meant to *demonstrate* quite so much."

Having felt so embarrassed about so many things herself tonight, Laela smiled warmly at her teacher. "I'm glad you did. I feel…more prepared now than I did just a few moments ago."

Aris returned the smile, but still appeared uneasy. "Well, I'm glad for that. Yet I should…conclude our lesson for this evening before I…"

"Before you what?"

The pretty young teacher shook her head. "Nothing," she said, her eyes drifting over Laela's bare curves as she hurriedly got to her feet and pulled her skirt down. "But I shall see you again tomorrow night, Laela, for our next lesson."

THE FOLLOWING EVENING, as dusk shadowed the air outside Laela's window, a knock came on her door. Hurrying to whisk it open, expecting to see Aris on the other side, she was surprised to find her oldest sister, Maven, who had not yet departed the fortress for her home in the north. Her eyes looked as big and round as the goblets they drank from at meals. "I have news," she said, taking Laela's hands.

Pushing her way in, she shut the door firmly behind her, then turned to face Laela. "Ogran is here. He's arrived early. Father has moved up the Giving Ceremony to tomorrow morning at sunrise!"

Laela gasped as a bolt of panic shot through her. "Oh no!"

Their father had done the same to Tecsia when she had been promised to Ralen. So much for royal tradition! And she supposed that, in the end, maybe it didn't matter much, a difference of one or two days, but she wasn't ready to go yet—she was scheduled for two more nights of Orientation with Aris, and after last night, she'd found herself looking forward to them. Certainly more, anyway, than she was looking forward to leaving with Ogran for "the mountains".

"And this very minute," Maven went on, out of

breath, "Father has the staff preparing a feast to greet him, and he summons you to join them for dinner."

At this, Laela simply sneered. It was bad enough to be betrothed to a man old enough to be her father's father, bad enough that she had to go off and share a home with him, but it was downright *humiliating* to have to eat with him in front of all the fort's inhabitants, reminding them all of the doom she was about to face.

For a second, she considered refusing outright—but one did not refuse Enrick, Ruler of Caralon. So she simply released a put-upon sigh and said, "Very well. Can you help me dress?" Normally, her maid Nila would have been called for this task, but she needed her sister just now.

Maven selected an emerald-colored frock of silk from Laela's wardrobe to match the green ribbon choker that always adorned Laela's neck these days, at its center an expensive metal medallion of a cat's face, with green eyes just like Midnight's. Her mother had commissioned the piece for her recent birthday, indulging her unusual affinity for such creatures. Although why they were bothering with something so trivial as matching a dress with a ribbon for a wretched old man, she had no idea.

Maven continued to talk incessantly, something Laela herself was usually famous for doing, but the last few days had quieted her. And rather than pay any attention to whatever Maven was chattering about at the moment—something about focusing on the future and the estate she would own once Ogran died—instead she simply tried to think positive thoughts to prepare herself for her impending marriage.

When I am forced to have sex with Ogran, I'll just think of my fantasy lover from the village.

And who knew—maybe Ogran was too *old* to fuck. Aris had said it took stamina.

And maybe she *would* take a lover—maybe Ogran would be too old and senile to even realize it. For she *wanted* a lover now, after having learned about sex. She wanted to know what it was to have a man inside her, she wanted that union—just not with *Ogran.*

A few short minutes later, Maven accompanied her toward the great hall, Laela taking deep, calming breaths, determined to be brave, for there seemed no other choice. But when they neared the entrance, she couldn't quite make herself go in. "Go on without me," she told her sister. "I'll be along in a moment."

The truth was, she was afraid of what she would find. She hadn't seen Ogran since she was a child and didn't have a firm memory of what he'd looked like even then. She wanted to prepare herself further now that the moment was at hand.

"Are you sure?" Maven asked, eyes doubtful, but Laela nodded, prodding her sister through the arched stone doorway.

Then she stood up straight, took one last deep breath, and was trying to convince herself maybe this would not be so bad, when she heard someone say, "Yes, Ogran, I've seen the girl and she's quite pretty indeed."

Lingering just beyond the door, Laela drew back slightly, given how close the voice was, then peeked around to find the middle-aged man who'd just spoken, a dark-haired fellow she didn't know, standing with… Dear Ares!—she'd known Ogran was old, but the sight of the elderly man was nearly too much to take! Small and slump-shouldered, the only hair on his head shone sparse and white—a rim of it just above his ears. His wrinkles sagged toward the pot belly that draped over the belt at his hips. She nearly fainted, and only reaching to press her palm to the cool rock wall next to her kept her from it.

The old man chuckled lecherously. "I can't wait to get my hands on her. It's been a great while since I took a virgin. I always enjoyed virgins in particular—so easy to show them who's in control. Every now and then you find a feisty one, but those are even more fun to tame. Just have to be a little rougher with them, but that's hardly a sacrifice." His beady eyes narrowed. "*Is* she feisty?"

The other man appeared amused by the old man, which turned Laela's stomach even more sour. "I'm unsure, but either way, she'll soon be yours to do with whatever you please."

Laela felt frozen in place, too shocked to move.

But only for a second. Because it took only that long for one thing to become indisputably clear in her mind.

She could not marry this elderly brute. *Could* not and *would* not.

Which left her only one recourse.
She had to run away.
And she had to do it now.

CHAPTER TWO

S TARK FEAR NIPPED at Laela's heels as she dashed up the beach, the fortress walls just barely visible behind her over the dunes. She took only a brief glance back as her bare feet slashed into the cool night sand, one after the other, propelling her forward. She could scarcely believe she was running away into the unknown, but after the ugly remarks she'd heard Ogran make, she felt safer leaving behind everything she knew than she would becoming his wife—and essentially, his property.

Thank goodness Donnell had let her pass—he'd been her only hope of leaving the fortress unnoticed, so it was lucky she'd known where he stood guard. He'd been hesitant, of course, worried for her safety, but she'd taken his hands, beseeched him with her eyes, and said, "I must leave, Donnell! I must! I cannot marry that terrible old wretch!" and finally he'd stepped aside, but not before lowering a kiss to her forehead and wishing her good luck.

Evening had fallen completely now and as she looked

out to sea, only the whitecaps on the waves could be seen. Up ahead, to her left, torches beckoned—the village of Myrtell.

Of course, she'd never been to the town alone before—never in her whole life. Royal girls were too closely guarded. And she'd certainly never been there at night. What had always struck her as a quaint, friendly community by daylight suddenly appeared a bit more ominous under the cover of darkness.

Still, she saw no other option but to enter the village. If her absence had not yet been discovered at the fortress, it would be any moment now. And while Myrtell was probably the first place her father's men would look, there would be more places to hide there than on the empty beach or the open ground surrounding the village. She wished she'd had time to form some better sort of plan than this one—but she simply hadn't, so now she had to make it up as she went.

Nearing Myrtell, she veered up away from the beach, running toward the enclave of huts and small buildings. Despite the torchlight, she soon discovered that the town was mostly quiet—doors shut, shutters pulled and businesses closed for the evening. It made her fear that a good place to hide might be harder to come by than she'd imagined, and a fresh shot of dread swirled through her.

She continued running, running, up the twisting commonways, between the structures of thatch and wood and stone, until a bit of laughter caught her ear.

She headed toward it and soon heard the sounds of more and more people. She knew instinctively she'd located her best chance of not being found.

Bursting from between two small huts, she came upon a brightly lit building, its walls constructed of thick planks of wood, its roof thatched, like most in the village. Above the open door hung a wooden sign with the word *Tavern* painted upon it, featuring a depiction of a goblet for those who didn't read.

Talk and laughter and even the sound of some sort of instrument spilled from the door and windows of the larger-than-average structure, and Laela knew it was her only hope. Trepidation bit at her at the prospect of entering a room full of strange men imbibing ale—but when, in the distance, she heard the sound of hooves, her father's horses, she sprinted toward the entrance and ducked inside.

She was stopped cold by the scene that met her eyes. Yes, the room was filled to bursting with men who held large goblets in their fists, but in the center of them all, on a long, wooden table, two women—bared to the waist—kissed each other passionately, clearly for the delight of the crowd! One leisurely caressed the other's large, round breasts and somewhere in the room a man let out an enthusiastic howl.

Laela's heartbeat, which had been frantic enough already, now escalated into something wild and out of control. She'd never seen anything like this before—she didn't even know two women could desire each other that way, nor that men would enjoy it so much!

"That's right, girls, nice and slow. Make it last."

The hot, raspy voice drew her gaze across the room to a dark-haired fellow probably around her own age, his equally dark eyes glued to the women.

But Laela's focus immediately shifted to the man at his side, for it was her handsome, sandy-haired fantasy lover! She nearly lost her breath at the sight of him, and even in the midst of her fear, her pussy went warm. Oh, to know *that* man as a wife knew a husband! To fuck him. She still didn't quite know what it *was* to fuck, but already she burned to do it with *him*.

"Oh yes, girls, keep going," the dark-haired young man said again, and Laela's eyes returned to the center of the tavern where now one of the women licked the other's nipple, dark pink and shiny with moisture. Both purred and moaned their pleasure, and everything around Laela—from the bare-breasted women to her fantasy lover to the hungry-eyed men whose musky scents hung all around her in the shadowy air—made her body hum with a tense excitement she'd never known.

"Good of you to provide such titillating entertainment, Garon!" a voice bellowed merrily from somewhere to Laela's right.

Her blond fantasy lover gave a short laugh. "I only pay them to serve the ale. But can I stop them if they wish to seek their pleasure between filling goblets?"

His dark-haired companion let out a guffaw. "We all know better than that, my friend."

More masculine laughter buffeted the room, reminding Laela how out of place she was here—the only woman in the room not engaging in a sexual act for the patrons' enjoyment.

She tried to digest it all. Garon—his name was Garon. And he owned the tavern? Yes, he must. But as to what exactly he paid the women for…no one elaborated on that further, leaving her to wonder. Something dark and forbidden stirred low in her belly as she tried to decipher an answer.

That's when she heard the thunder of hooves nearby, even above the tavern noises. Her father's horses were the only such animals anywhere in the vicinity, so she knew his men, too, were headed toward the torches and laughter, searching for her! And she'd wasted precious minutes being shocked and aroused and not doing anything to save herself. "Pardon me, excuse me," she said, suddenly pushing her way through the throng of men surrounding her.

"What do we have here?" a particularly burly fellow nearly twice her size asked as he closed a hand around her shoulder.

Suddenly, there was no *time* for fear, so she only glared at the big beast. "I must reach Garon. Unhand me!"

The man flinched, letting go, and she pushed through the crowded room toward the handsome blond man whose sparkling blue eyes were now locked on hers. Of course, it seemed *lots* of men's eyes were suddenly devouring her—even choosing to ogle *her* over the tawdry sight in the middle of the room—but she focused only on her fantasy lover. Not only was there no time for fear, there was no time for indulging her lust or shyness at the moment, either.

Garon couldn't have been more intrigued by the pretty little nymph making her way toward him through the crush of men filling his tavern. He'd never seen anyone appear more out of place—she looked like a bright, lone flower in a field of mud and grime. He knew instantly she was wealthy—the silk dress gave her away. And he knew she was innocent, too—the braid falling down her back told *that* tale.

"You must hide me," she insisted vehemently as she reached him.

He quirked an unhurried smile. "From what, princess?"

Just then, he heard the whinny of horses being drawn to a rough halt outside—rare and valuable enough animals that he knew only one man who owned any. Enrick, their ruler.

"My father's men," she said, and he couldn't help noticing how her hazel eyes nearly matched those in the odd cat's-head pendant worn at her throat.

He narrowed his gaze on her, sizing her up. So she was Enrick's daughter—the last of them yet to marry, if he remembered correctly. If he had any sense, he'd turn the girl over to the men without a second thought.

But her eyes were so frightened. And she *was* a pretty

little nymph. He crossed his arms and leaned his head back slightly. "What's in it for *me*?"

Her eyes grew even rounder than they already appeared, and she looked lost for an answer. Finally, she said, "What do you want?"

Garon wished he had more time to weigh his reply, but he knew the men were going to burst in the door looking for this lovely girl any moment now. He gave her a long once-over, reminding himself he could be put to death for crossing the great ruler of Caralon. To even *consider* it was pure folly.

"Anything you want from me, it's yours," she said hurriedly, frantically. "So long as my father's men don't find me."

"Your body," he said plainly.

"What?" She looked aghast at the suggestion, her gaze going wide.

But Garon only laughed. "Take it or leave it, princess."

She drew in her breath sharply, then spoke through slightly clenched teeth. "Fine. Fine, whatever you want. Just hide me!"

He gave her his most lecherous, satisfied grin, along with a little nod of agreement, then spoke to the fellow standing next to him without ever letting his gaze leave hers. "Baelor, take her to my room and make sure she's well hidden. And, uh, be sure she stays there—I don't want her deciding to leave before I get payment for my…services."

Baelor let out a low chuckle, clamping his warm hand around her wrist and pulling her deeper into the tavern—and Garon wondered what in Ares' name he'd just done, and more importantly, why. Hadn't he just lectured himself about folly?

Seconds later, a handful of large warrior types came bounding through the door so roughly that even Sima and Janya, his two tavern maids, looked up from where they sat entangled in each other's soft bodies, their leather skirts now raised to their hips, their breasts pressed lightly together.

But he couldn't take more than a quick glimpse at the sumptuous sight of them—he had much bigger business to attend to.

"It's not often we see men from Enrick's fortress here. What can I do for you? Ale?" Then he motioned to Sima and Janya, letting a lecherous smile form on his face. "Or maybe you'd prefer women?"

The largest man stepped forward. "You own this tavern?"

He gave a friendly nod, then introduced himself. "Garon of Myrtell."

"We're looking for a girl. Brown hair—"

Again, he motioned toward the barely clad ladies in his employ. "Right here. *Two* attractive girls who would be happy to please you in any way you can think of for a mere bit of metal or a few colored stones." That was how he sold his ale—for bits of the most valued materials in Caralon, which he could then barter for whatever he needed. Slowly, he was amassing more and more of the stuff, becoming a rather rich man for a mere villager.

The big warrior simply looked impatient. "We're looking for a *particular* young woman. Brown braided hair, hazel eyes, wearing a green frock. Has she been here?"

Garon slowly looked around the room, where all eyes now watched the scene near the door. "As you can see, our customers here are strictly of the male variety. So unless either of those two lovely vixens on the table are the one you're seeking, I'm afraid I can't help you."

The warrior didn't move or speak for a moment, as if he didn't quite believe Garon. But Garon stood his ground. They had no reason to suspect him other than his establishment being only one of few open after darkness fell in Myrtell. "A lot of places a girl could hide out there in the dark," he said easily, motioning beyond the walls of the tavern. "And if the girl you described had come in here…well, I think I'd have noticed her, don't you?"

Slowly, Enrick's head man seemed to relax, his companions following his lead. "I guess we'd better get back to the search," he said to them.

Garon gave a somber nod. "Good luck to you."

The large fellow nodded briefly in return, then herded his small band back out the open door into the night. The string player in the corner slowly began strumming a sensual tune once more and it seemed a cue for the tavern to resume activity. Sima and Janya smiled at each other and exchanged a sensual tongue kiss that lifted his cock. Or maybe it was on the rise for some entirely *different* reason. A reason that waited in his bedchamber this very second.

Rather than head back there just now, though, he waited. Reached for his goblet and took a long swallow of sweet, grainy ale. Watched his customers delight over the female entertainment. Looked back to the girls to see darkly-complexioned Sima recline Janya across the wooden table and ease her way down generous curves, kissing Janya's stomach, then parting her legs to reveal hair as red as that which adorned her head. Pink flesh jutted from between and every man's gaze was riveted, waiting for Sima to lick it.

It was a performance Garon had seen many times, but he never tired of it.

Part of him couldn't quite believe he'd just put his life on the line by lying to Enrick's men about—dear Ares—the ruler's daughter. He was actually harboring a royal runaway. Worse yet, one who still possessed the bride price between her legs. And he'd told her he wanted her *body*? What had he been thinking?

Well, it was more what his cock had been thinking, he supposed. He'd suffered the same reaction he would have to *any* pretty girl. Only he should have ignored it this time.

Turn her out now and you might still get out of this alive.

Yes, that was what any sane man would do.

He didn't know why she was hiding, but he'd made the mistake of agreeing to help her, and now—not from kindness, but from a healthy sense of self-preservation—he was going to deny himself the enticing curves he'd seen under that shimmering green fabric and send her on her way.

As soon as he watched Sima and Janya eat each other's delectable cunts, that was. He'd never been very skilled at denying himself anything when it came to women.

LAELA LAY FLAT on her back beneath the bed where Baelor had unceremoniously shoved her. She couldn't hear anything through the door other than muffled voices. Her skin prickled—from the raw fear of being discovered, and also from the deal she'd made with her fantasy lover. Garon.

A fantasy not for very much longer, it would seem. Soon she would know what it was to fuck him. The thought shriveled her fear a bit, and transformed her tension into anticipation. Even lying in the dark, under the bed, her body still tingled, her breasts aching pleasantly with want and her cunt seeming to tickle.

He was just as handsome as she remembered. Dark blond hair fell over his forehead and down onto his neck, dimples shone in his cheeks when he cast those wicked little smiles of his, and she'd never been close enough before to see the scintillating sparkle in his eyes, but it had nearly been enough to bury her.

In one way, she couldn't quite believe what she'd agreed to, yet in another, it had been easy. Yes, she was nervous about their arrangement, but if she was honest with herself, she felt equally as excited. Sex with Garon might even be enough to take her mind off the fact that she'd just run away from the most powerful man in Caralon and left behind every ounce of the existence she'd known up to now.

Her mind played over Garon's deep, confident voice calling her *princess*. She'd never actually heard the archaic term for a royal girl spoken aloud. It was a rare word, known to few, only those well read in the older texts of the Before Times. How did the tavern keeper even *know* such a word?

As seconds stretched into minutes, her mind wandered. What would it be like to have him on top of her, to have his hands on her breasts, his mouth on hers? What would his cock be like? For that matter, what was *any* cock like? Aris' drawings were good, but so two-dimensional—Laela still had little notion of what to expect.

Her musings calmed her...until a hand closed around her ankle.

She let out a small screech.

"Quiet." It was Baelor, sounding annoyed. "I think the men are gone, but we don't need your squeals bringing them back." With that, he tugged on her leg, trying to pull her out from under the bed.

"Ow, you're hurting me. I can get out myself."

The young man released her from his grasp and she eased her way from beneath the bed to sit up. Kneeling next to her, he smiled, and it was the first time she noticed that Garon was not the only handsome man in this building. Baelor's cheeks were dusted with dark stubble and his eyes glittered a steely gray. She caught a glimpse of dark hair curling on his chest, visible beneath an open leather vest. The warmth from her previous ponderings increased, spreading all through her at his nearness. "Garon likes feisty women," he said.

Despite her new awareness of him, she only rolled her eyes, recalling that so did Ogran. "That seems to be the general consensus in Myrtell."

"I do, too," he informed her, "so you're lucky Garon already has a claim on you."

She raised her eyebrows. "Is that so? I don't suppose *my* feelings on this matter at all?"

He laughed. "You're funny, too. Garon is lucky." He pushed to his feet, then went to rummage in a cabinet near the hearth. "And just so you know—no, I would not take you against your will. I would simply seduce you."

This made *her* laugh, and his tone said he didn't mind, that he was teasing her a bit. She found herself surprisingly drawn to him, so much so that she wished she'd paid more attention to his touches on her wrist earlier, and just now, on her ankle. She experienced a vague urge to touch *him*.

Until he turned back around and said, "Lie down on the bed."

She tensed, her cunt flinching. "Why?"

He looked perturbed. "You heard Garon tell me to make sure you didn't leave. Now lie down."

Pulling in her breath at this sudden change of tone, she obeyed the command, then watched—in a combination of shock and horror—as Baelor brought two strips of leather to the bedstead and methodically tied first one of her wrists to the right post, then the other to the left. "Wh-what are you…?"

He gave her a matter-of-fact look, then enunciated very clearly, as if she might be slow-minded. "Making sure you don't *leave*. Remember?"

She let out a sigh. Seemed she'd somehow gone from one type of captivity to another.

Even so, whatever happened here, it was by far preferable to what would have happened to her with Ogran. That thought made the bindings a little more bearable, even as they pulled tight at her skin and thrust her breasts forward against the silk of her dress. She couldn't help wondering if Baelor noticed her nipples jutting through the green fabric, and—although she scarcely knew why, for Garon was the object of her affections—she almost hoped he did, and hoped that he liked it. The thought made her pussy moist.

She couldn't help being pleased when his eyes raked boldly over her—even as he headed toward the door to depart. He flashed another impish grin. "Have a fun evening, virgin girl."

She gasped at the reminder—and as the door shut behind him, she wished she'd hidden her reaction better. Here in town by herself, outside the fortress, she'd already forgotten her braid and what it signified to those who saw her. At home, she was accustomed to it—and no one there gave it a second thought. In the village, though, where most girls shed their virginity long before reaching royal bride's age, she supposed the braid was like a sign suspended from her neck. *Royal Virgin. Total Innocent. Never Been Fucked.*

Laela lay tied to the bed then for what seemed like hours. Her mind raced the whole time, never slowing. She remembered the two women in the other room, kissing and undressing one another while the men watched, and she wondered what might be happening now. With each sound of laughter or collective lusty sigh through the door, she couldn't resist wondering just what exactly she was missing, and what part Garon might play in it. For with Baelor's departure, her mind had turned again to her fantasy lover, the man she'd promised her body to.

Odd, now that she'd met him, he seemed more an enigma than ever.

And the longer she lay there—worrying about her father's anger, or that his men could return, worrying about what her life would become now—the more she wanted Garon to come for her. Not only did she desperately want the distraction from her worrisome thoughts—she also wanted to learn the mysteries of sex from a man, once and for all. The sights and sensations of the evening had built in her an entirely new sort of desire—something brazen and hungry that couldn't be pushed down. Were her hands not tied, she would have touched herself to ease the hot ache. Blasted strips of leather.

Finally, when her cunt felt near implosion and she'd nearly given up on his ever coming through the door—it opened. In the outer room, soft laughter and the clink of goblets could still be heard, but she had the sense of a smaller, quieter crowd now that the night had grown later. She lay, her arms stretched to either side, watching as he entered the shadowy chamber.

Baelor had left large candles burning, and Garon's blue eyes sparkled in the light when he delivered a wicked smile. "Waiting up for me, princess? How sweet."

She pursed her lips at his roguish manner. "It's a bit difficult to sleep while trussed like a pig."

He chuckled. "Come now, you're hardly tied up *that* well. But if you'd like me to try, I can get more leather."

She simply blinked. "Why would I…?"

He let out another of his knowing little laughs. "Some women like to be bound very tight, princess."

She flinched slightly, just then understanding that he must be talking about something sexual. "Oh. Well…I don't believe I'm one of them. In fact, my arms hurt."

"If you ask *me*, you look damnably tempting that way." He walked slowly around the bed, giving her a long once-over. Her body hummed under his scrutiny, her breasts feeling even more sensitive and needy beneath his gaze and her pussy tingling madly, even if some unexamined instinct led her to draw her legs together beneath her silken gown. She liked his eyes on her, yet at the same time, they made her feel all too vulnerable. "Indeed, a man could be tempted to shove up those fancy skirts and sink his cock into your royal cunt, princess."

Heat climbed her cheeks as the truth assaulted her—he had full control here. She'd known that before, of course, but only now did the true measure of her helplessness strike her. He could do whatever he wished and there was nothing she could do to stop him.

But if she suffered any fear, it was tempered with desire—the desire she'd always felt for him, the desire that had burned slowly hotter all night as she'd awaited him—so she shoved her worries aside and tried to be bold. "Only *tempted*?" She pushed her lower lip out, pouting slightly, trying to look sensual, ready to be a willing, wanting woman for him.

He stood at the foot of the bed, arms crossed, looking at once aroused and amused, until finally that same devilish smile she'd seen before crept over his handsome face. "Yes, only tempted, princess." Then he slowly stepped up to the headboard and began untying one wrist. "And I'm afraid you'll have to leave now."

Even the touch of his rough fingertips on her tender skin was exciting, but his words left her dumbfounded.

What was he saying? "What do you mean? I thought you wanted my body in exchange for hiding me."

When the leather strip loosened, freeing her wrist, she drew her aching arm to her side and watched as Garon circled around to begin unknotting the other tie. "I do. But unfortunately, I can't have it."

As her other arm dropped to her side, tired and heavy, she bit her lip, trying to understand. "Why not?" She feared she sounded terribly disappointed, but forced herself to continue. "Because…well, it's not so much that I wish you to have it, but we made a deal—you did hide me, and so I'm indebted to you now. I…would not feel right if I did not pay that debt."

That familiar grin reappeared as he hovered over her. "Indeed, you are indebted to me—and you have no idea how much I would enjoy finding out just how warm and tight that virgin pussy of yours is, but…you're a bit too dangerous for me."

She sat up a little more. "Dangerous? Me?"

Again, he crossed his arms. "If I sank my shaft between those slender thighs and your father found out, what do you think he'd do to me?"

Oh. She hadn't thought about that. And though the answer was obvious, she only mumbled, "I don't know."

"Well, I do. He'd probably cut my cock off. Or my head. Either way, that's not a chance I'm willing to take, even for a ripe and royal little cunt like yours."

"It has no hair," she said. She wasn't sure *why* she said it, only that she wanted him to know. If he wasn't going to fuck her, she wanted him to know what he was missing and be sorry he was missing it.

"What?" he asked, blinking.

She swallowed, nervous now that she'd brought up such an intimate—and perhaps bizarre—topic. "It was…all removed. For my wedding."

He seemed to stand up a little straighter, his mouth cutting a grim line across his face as he held up a hand. "Stop, wait. Your *what*?"

"My, uh, wedding."

Garon let out a long sigh and ran one hand back through his sandy hair.

"But don't worry, I didn't get married." She sat up still more, began massaging one wrist, where the leather had been, then the other. "And I'm not going to. At least not to *that* man."

"That man?" he asked, sounding matter-of-fact even if slightly more worried than just a moment ago.

Trying to think how best to explain, she let out a sigh of her own. "My father promised me to an old man. A *very* old man. And I was going to try to go through with it, but then I saw him, and I heard him talking about me—and I just *couldn't*. So…I ran."

"Here," he said, seeking clarification.

"There was no time to form a plan."

He sat down on the edge of the bed, blinking slowly, his gaze calmer now. "Makes sense, I suppose," he said, then slowly let his expression transform into something more naughty. "But now, back to your cunt. They removed the hair?"

She nodded. "I'm told men like it that way."

His eyes stuck on hers, sizzling like blue flames, and they simply looked at each other for a long, smoldering moment. She'd never wanted to be so close to fire—but she definitely wanted to get closer to *him*, even if meant she might get burned.

The stubble on his cheek made her want to touch, run her hands over his face, feel the roughness on her fingertips. The light sheen of perspiration on his skin made her want to soak him into her. And those eyes— they were melting her, melting her down and making her into something entirely new. He was so real, so raw, so unlike any man she'd ever encountered in the fortress. No riches or lands or wealthy families to turn him arrogant. A simple working man with calluses on his hands. And an utterly *sexual* man with fire in his eyes.

"Do...*you* like it that way?" she asked of her denuded pussy, her voice coming out low, slightly husky.

He cast a slow, intoxicating grin. "I don't know. I've never had the pleasure of seeing one in such a condition."

She felt short of breath, and her words came out sparse and labored as coarse desire turned her shockingly wanton. "Do you want to see...mine?"

CHAPTER THREE

L AUGHTER TOUCHED HIS eyes before it left his throat, then seemed to crash over her, killing the quiet tension. "I certainly do, princess, but…"

"But?" she prodded when he trailed off.

He arched one eyebrow. "I'm not sure I could resist that kind of temptation."

Laela barely knew what came over her then, but she wanted that thick, heated tension *back*. She wanted to feel the warmth moving between them, like something you could reach out and touch, grab, as she'd felt it a moment ago. Her body thrummed with needing more—needing this man to show her everything she yearned to know, give her everything she wanted to feel—and she wasn't going to let him laugh and tease it away.

No, she was going to do what Baelor had mentioned earlier. She was going to *seduce* Garon.

She sensually licked her lips, lowered her chin provocatively, and let him see the longing in her gaze. "I want to show you."

Surprise sparked in his eyes, and she liked catching him off guard. "Why?"

It seemed a time for honesty. "I've…seen you before. Here, in the village. I've thought you…very handsome—a man I wished to…know more of."

His eyes slowly began to glitter with curiosity, and she could tell she'd flattered him. The delicious tension she'd craved had indeed just returned and seemed to be spilling over them like something slow and syrupy.

"All right then, princess," he said, his voice low. "Show me."

Laela shifted and rose to her knees on the bed beside him. Garon peered intently at her face, then let his gaze sink lower, over her breasts, to her hips. She was starting to perspire, but not from the warm Myrtell night. Her skin felt slick, her whole body hot.

Her fingers curled into the soft silk that cascaded down her thighs until she made fists—fists that gathered fabric, then more fabric, and more. When her knees were bared to him and her pussy tingled so wet and hungry she thought she might die of it, she pushed down the last vestiges of shyness still lurking inside her. Slowly, she lifted the draping silk higher, the heat in the room seeming to climb with each inch the dress ascended. By the time she clutched the fabric at the very tops of her thighs, she feared she might be dripping from the anticipation.

More of that enticing fire flashed in his gaze, now riveted on the juncture of her thighs.

Wetter. His intense look made her wetter and wetter.

Finally, she took a deep breath and raised the folds of the gown to her waist, putting herself fully on display for this man of her fantasies, this stranger she wanted so badly.

He simply stared at her pussy, heavy-lidded. She could feel his arousal falling around her like a warm winter fur.

Swallowing back the lump of excitement in her throat, she barely found her voice. "Do you like it?"

It took a moment for him to raise his eyes back to hers. "Oh yes." A deep rasp.

The words trickled through her like a low rumble of thunder and she dealt out another dare—for both of them. "Touch it."

His eyes had dropped back to her cunt, but now flew to hers. Sensual amusement danced within. "Naughty little princess, aren't you?"

Finding she rather liked the accusation, she let a playful smile admit it. "I want you," she said, low and clear.

"*Naughty,*" he whispered as he reached up to cup her smooth mound in the palm of his hand—a warm vise that deluged her with still more of that flooding wetness. "*Naughty.*" He drew his fingers forward, letting one dip deliciously into her moisture. "*Naughty.*" He finished by swirling his fingertips over her clit, resulting in a hot burst of pleasure that radiated outward.

But then he drew back, removing his oh-so-welcome

touch, and Laela suffered the niggling fear that she'd somehow failed in her seduction attempt—and she simply couldn't. She *had* to have him. *Tonight.* "You're not going to leave me this way, are you?" she asked with a pout.

His eyes narrowed on her, more serious now, but his gaze remained thick with lust. "You must want to see me dead for some reason, princess. Because that's what will happen if I take your bride price."

She shook her head vehemently. "He will never know. Because I'm not going back. Even if they *drag* me back, I'll run away again. I'm my own woman now…and I want you to fuck me."

She watched Garon pull in his breath, seeming to consider her words, to weigh it all.

The desire that burned low in her core mixed with the nervous churning of her stomach. "I'll ask you again. You're not going to leave me like this, are you?"

He let out a sigh, but his blue eyes still blazed with the same want that sizzled relentlessly through *her* body. Finally, he said, "No, princess. I'm not going to leave you like this."

Reaching up to steady his hands over the silk at her waist, he lowered her back onto the bed and parted her thighs in one smooth move. His face hovered just above her exposed cunt, so close his breath warmed it, and Laela's heartbeat kicked up with the sudden realization that she wasn't really sure what would happen now. The situation had shifted in the space of a heartbeat, and suddenly her Orientation with Aris seemed woefully lacking. "Wh-what…?" she began brokenly, lost. She didn't even know what she wanted to ask.

And she never drew a conclusion, since that's when he blew on her clit and stroked his fingers through the wetness below. It was as if lightning had just struck her cunt—*hot, thrilling* lightning, like a gift from Ares above. She whimpered at the unanticipated pleasure arcing through her.

"Whoever said men liked it without hair was right, princess," he rasped up at her. "What a beautiful pussy you have." His big fingers stroked into her again, making her moan. How could one mere touch travel so far, up into her breasts, tingling out through her arms and legs?

"I'm…glad you like it," she said, her voice coming out breathy. "So, so glad. It…likes you, too."

He let out a full-bodied laugh, then met her gaze, suddenly looking mischievous. "Then it's about to like me a whole lot better."

She drew in her breath at the promise, clenching lightly between her legs.

His voice went infinitely softer, whispering, "Relax."

She bit her lip slightly, then tried to follow the command, letting her body loosen beneath the warmth of his beside her.

And then his fingers came again, pressing, swimming in the slit that she could see lay open and pink and glistening now beneath his caress. She heard her own breath grow thready as she watched, soaking up the sensation of those rough, firm fingers that managed to touch her so gently.

When he twirled her clit between thumb and forefinger, she squealed with the shocking delight of it and found herself curling her fingers tight into the bed furs at each side of her. "Oh…" she said. She meant to say more, but what? There were no words for such pleasure.

"Such a pretty pussy, princess," he cooed, his breath still warm on her cunt.

For some reason, the simple compliment seemed to lift her higher still, to a place where nothing else mattered *but* her pussy. It seemed the most prominent part of her, the place on her body that defined her whole being in this moment. That quickly, Garon had turned her into…sex. Just sex. She was sex and nothing more as he touched her. And it was all she wanted to be.

His hand slid downward then, his longest finger stroking through her fleshy folds, raking, raking, showing her joys she'd never known, then touching deeper, even deeper, until—Oh Ares!—his finger plied at her, pushing, almost digging, making her want to somehow open to him more than she already had. And then she remembered Aris' pointer and how it had entered her— in the very same spot where he stroked so deep and relentlessly.

His finger sank inward, inside her, and she released a soft cry.

"How's that, princess?" he asked in that same deep, husky voice of sex.

A shaky "Good" was all she could muster.

"It's about to get better," he quipped, sounding amused with himself just before he blew on her clit once more and then—Ares above!—sank his mouth there.

Oh! She couldn't have imagined such deep, thrilling delights as those that assaulted her now. Aris had told her a man liked to have a woman use her mouth on his cock, but she'd had no idea the reverse was possible, nor so incredible!

She watched, panting, as Garon's tongue moved sensually over the little pink nub of flesh at the top of her slit. Each lick vibrated through her like something mystical, magical. And when Garon shifted his gaze from his work to her eyes—oh, she'd never experienced such an intimate connection with anyone in her life!

His finger still pressed into her below, moving in and out, just like Aris' pointer had, but his finger was warmer, softer, more welcome there. Without planning it, her hips began to move—she lifted her pussy to his hand, to his mouth, wanting more and more of his tongue and lips and teeth there. It was like touching herself, but better—because it came from *him*, this amazing man with fiery eyes and a mouth that was taking her straight to heaven.

Soon enough, she knew she would find that heaven that felt so near—and nothing else mattered. She let go of the bed furs and instead coiled her fingers into his hair, massaging his scalp, pulling him to her where she thrummed and ached and needed him most. He sucked her clit between his teeth as he moved his finger—maybe more than one now?—inside her, and she moaned at each rhythmic touch and lick, and felt her pleasure climbing, climbing…until she reached that astounding summit of release. "Oh Ares! Oh Ares! Yes!" Uncontrollable sobs left her as the sensation pounded through her like the hot beat of a drum, and she closed her eyes, seeing nothing but darkness and delicious joy as finally the orgasm faded.

A feather-soft kiss—laced with an odd, sweet taste that she thought must have come from her cunt—touched her lips. By the time she tried to kiss back, though, he was gone.

Slowly, she opened her eyes and met Garon's. "I've never…felt anything so perfect."

He gave a slight grin, although his eyes still looked serious. "I'm glad you liked it, princess."

She could scarcely believe this had happened—with *this* man, her fantasy man from the village—but now she wanted more. "Take off your clothes and fuck me," she begged.

Yet Garon only gave his head a skeptical tilt—then got up and walked toward the door without looking back.

Shock and disappointment roared through her, becoming physical reactions as well as emotional ones. "You're not going to fuck me?"

He faced her with a cynical laugh, although his words seemed laced with kindness. "No, princess, I'm afraid you and I are done here."

For a second, Laela couldn't breathe. Why was he leaving? How could he not want what *she* wanted? She had to stop him from going. How could she save this? Desperation brought an answer. "My Orienter told me it was difficult, once you're aroused, to sleep that way."

"That's why I made you come," he replied, one eyebrow arching.

"I was…thinking of you."

He slyly lowered his chin. "Don't worry—I *won't* be sleeping that way. Surely you saw Sima and Janya when you came in."

The two women kissing in the tavern. "Oh…" More disappointment, this time paired with stark jealousy, rushed through her like a bitter drink of water. Someone else would have his cock tonight. Maybe even *two* someone elses. It wasn't fair—or right. She still wanted, urgently, to somehow draw him back to her. "Wait. Before you go…"

He cynically arched one brow. "Yes?"

"Show me your cock. I haven't yet seen one. I want to see it."

Garon's desire seemed to reach out from his hungry shaft in hard, clawing fingers that tightened every muscle in his body. It was risky enough that he'd pleasured her, but he'd simply been unable to resist. And now the little nymph was begging to see his rod? He'd best get out of this room—quickly. "That…would be a bad idea."

"Why?"

He simply laughed. "You're relentless, aren't you?"

"When I need to be." She blinked coyly, and even that was almost enough to bury him. Ares, this girl was enticing—the way innocence and eagerness meshed in her hazel green eyes almost hypnotized him. "Show me," she said, a slight edge of demand in her voice that made his cock a little more rigid.

Taking a deep breath, Garon walked slowly back to the side of the bed where she lay. *This is a mistake. Turn around. Walk out the door right now. Let Sima and Janya take care of you.* Yet his feet kept moving toward the ruler's all-too-dangerous daughter.

When he reached her, he couldn't resist stroking his palm lightly up the bulge in his leather pants. He heard her sigh in anticipation as she lay in beautiful disarray beneath him, her green gown still falling around the tops of her shapely thighs. Her berry-colored lips lay parted in wonder and he couldn't help enjoying the power she awarded him in that moment—knowing what she wanted so badly, and that it was his to give.

He was tempted to tell *her* to unlace his pants if she wanted to see his shaft so badly—but no. He would do it himself, let her see his cock—and then, by Ares, he would get out of there before it was too late.

As he methodically worked the strained leather lacings, he remained all too aware that the girl before him was a virgin. It was the only way he could account for his uncharacteristic excitement at revealing himself to her. It was one thing with Sima, or Janya, or any of the other village women—they'd seen as many cocks as he'd seen cunts, it was nothing new. But for this girl, inexperienced and fresh as a spring day…somehow he almost felt like a virgin himself as he parted the opening of his pants and let his erection burst forth.

She gasped at the sight and he felt her awe trickle through him. He glanced down at the reddened head and the hard, veined column of flesh stretching stiffly beneath. Her first. He *wanted* to be her first. In more than just seeing his shaft.

Without warning, she reached up slender fingers to touch it. They raked ticklishly down over the skin like thin threads of heat. He tried not to let her see his pleasure, for that wouldn't aid his determination to resist her.

When she petted it as if it were an animal, he let out a hard sigh he wished he could have held in. Her simple touch was like fire. Next, she gingerly wrapped her hand full around it, squeezing lightly, and the sensation shot through him, making him moan.

She smiled. "You like to be touched here."

Her innocence drew another chuckle from him, despite himself. "Of course I do, princess. Touching works both ways, you know."

She nodded slowly, as if just starting to really figure that out.

Damnation, he wanted her so badly he couldn't breathe. If she'd just been a bit more shy, a little more hesitant, he could have easily been out the door by now—but her eagerness was proving downright irresistible. She wanted more of his cock, that was plain to see. Fortunately for Garon, there were ways to give it to her without taking her precious virginity. "Put it in your mouth, princess."

Her eyes widened even as she kept her small hand curled around his hard length. "Really?"

Did he detect a bit of nervousness in her voice? Maybe she'd be too afraid—and it would allow him to make his escape.

But instead she just asked, "Um…how exactly?"

A fresh burst of lust traveled the span of his body at the question—his little princess wasn't going shy at all, and now he no longer wanted her to. Reaching down, he ran one hand over the brown hair that led back to her virginal braid, and as the notion hit him that a virgin was going to suck his cock, it was nearly enough to make him explode right then and there.

"Just ease your lips down over it," he said softly, leaning toward her, watching as she rose up, bringing her face so enticingly close to his stiff, sensitive shaft. "Ease your lips down as far as you can, and then, if you like, move your head up and down, taking the cock in and out of your mouth."

Her lips were parted so prettily as she gazed up at him that he couldn't wait to see them wrapped around him below.

"Do it," he prodded in a barely audible whisper.

Re-situating herself to kneel on the bed, she gripped

him a little tighter, then bent to gently lick the tip, taking away the dot of moisture there. He groaned at the touch of her tongue, amazed at her lovely way of easing into the task, clearly following her Ares-given instincts on how to pleasure a man. His knees nearly gave out as she swirled her wet tongue all around the head and then slowly but purposefully sank her mouth over the end of his cock.

He let out a low sound of pleasure as the physical delight melded with the visual. Enrick's pretty virgin daughter was sucking his cock in his bedchamber, her braid falling forgotten over one shoulder, her full lips looking swollen and leaving a beautiful circle of wetness behind as she began to do what he'd instructed, moving up and down on him.

His breathing came in low rhythmic groans as he began to meet her movements with light thrusts. "Yes," he growled over her. "Yes, you're doing well, princess. So well. Don't stop. Don't stop."

His eager little virgin worked over him like she'd been delivering such treats for years. He stroked his thumbs over her cheeks, felt the stretch of the skin there, touched fingers to her lips where they circled him to feel the "O" her mouth made. Mostly, she worked with her eyes closed—but when she opened them wide to peer up at him and their gazes connected, hard and hot, he knew he didn't want to come this way with her.

No, he wanted between her legs. He wanted to know that soft, untried flesh opening just for him.

And indeed, he never *had* been very good at denying himself anything when it came to women.

"Ares," he bit off angrily, lost in lust and disgust at himself.

His princess looked up, releasing him from her tender mouth. "What?"

He couldn't let this go on—he had to stop it, once and for all. "You have to go. *Now.*" His hands still curved sensually about her head, making the moment all the more awkward.

She sat upright, disbelief turning her hazel eyes a dark shade of green that seemed to closer match those in the odd little cat's head pendant at her throat. "You're going to put me out, at night, in the dark?"

He released a sigh and let a matter-of-fact gruffness color his voice. "Sorry, princess, but if I don't, I'll take your virginity, and then what?"

"Well—"

He didn't give her a chance to answer. "I'll *tell* you what. You'll end up back at that fortress and when it's discovered your virginity is gone, you'll tell them who did it. And then I'll be dead."

She shook her head vehemently, the high braid swishing in back. "I won't, I swear it. And I told you—I don't intend to end up back at the fortress or ever even *near* anyone royal again."

He narrowed his gaze on her, doubtful. She sounded earnest, but she remained such an innocent—full of bravado, and he knew she had no idea how to survive outside the fortress walls. "And just where do you intend to go?"

She drew in a deep breath, eyes worried. "This all came up rather suddenly, as I explained, so I'm not sure. But…" She let out a tired sigh. "Couldn't I just stay here? I promise I won't be any trouble. I could…serve ale like Sima and Janya."

Garon tilted his head and released a dry chuckle, then replied with an edge in his voice to make sure she heard him, to make sure she understood the reality of existence in the village compared to life in her safe, sugar-coated fortress. "Princess, in case you haven't noticed, Sima and Janya serve more than ale. They enjoy their work, granted, but they get paid for what they like to do best, which is fuck. I don't need a tavern maid who just serves ale." With that, he turned to stalk away, to finally leave her there, as he should have done long before now.

But Ares help him, he couldn't do it. Just couldn't.

He wanted her too fervently, the need burning low in his belly, a sensation so desperate he couldn't quite understand it.

Because she was a virgin? No—it had to be more than that. It was because she was beautiful and ripe and fresh, at once hotter than the sun that blistered Myrtell's beaches in summer and sweeter than honey straight from the hive.

He'd obviously lost his mind, and his chest burned with anger at himself, and at her—for coming into his tavern and his life so unexpectedly, and seemingly stealing away his sanity.

Without thinking it through—for there *was* no thinking it through—he looked back and spoke brusquely. "Get this straight. If I do this, if I fuck you, you're *mine*. For as long as I want you to be. You're my slave, princess, in every way. What I say, you do. If I want you to serve ale, you serve ale. If I tell you to suck my cock, you suck it. Do you understand?"

For the first real time since they'd met, she looked a little frightened, as well she should. He *wanted* to scare her, wanted her to know there was a price to be paid for what she asked of him. Yet, even so, she never wavered as she answered, "Yes."

Making a slave of her was the only way Garon could turn this acceptable in his mind. She was too sweet, too exciting, and something about her made his heart feel stretched and twisted in his chest. If ever he was going to care about a woman again, this was *not* the one. So if he was going to fuck her, he was also going to *use* her. He was going to treat her like the sex toy she clearly wanted to be for him, and she'd likely be a damn good one. And if he *treated* her like a slave...well then, that was all she would *be* to him—nothing more.

"All right then," he said, deep and husky, glad the candles were burning a little lower than when he'd first come in the room, for he wanted the small chamber to feel as dark as this arrangement he'd just made with her, as dark as it felt in his soul. "Get ready, princess," he whispered. "Get ready, because there's no turning back now."

He crawled slowly toward her from the foot of the bed, getting closer, closer, moving up over her lithe young body, until he was straddling her, planting his knees astride her hips.

He hadn't seen her breasts yet, and he grazed slow, seeking hands from her shoulders down to capture the lush mounds in a firm yet gentle grip. Her gasp was one of pure pleasure—her nipples were hard pebbles jutting up against his palms through the fabric of her dress.

He hadn't really kissed her yet, either, despite his earlier intimacy with her delightfully swollen lips, so he bent, lowering his mouth full over hers. Awkward at first, her attempts clumsy, but then she managed to find the right rhythm and kiss him back, a kiss filled with all the heat that had been flowing between them since he'd first entered this room. He stroked his tongue between her lips and it seemed to take her aback. But soon enough she caught on to that, too, licking at it with her own, finding more natural pieces of her own sensuality and letting them out for his enjoyment.

One more thing he realized remained a mystery between them—he didn't know her name. She was Enrick's daughter—he *should* know, most people probably did. But he'd never paid attention to such things—royalty and wealth had never much interested him. "Tell me your name, princess," he asked between kisses, still molding her ample breasts in his hands.

"Laela," she said, the syllables flowing like something

liquid off her tongue.

"Pretty," he murmured against her lips. "Almost as pretty as the rest of you."

He wanted to get to her breasts, and was sorely tempted to rip the silk down the center, but he was a practical man, enough to realize this was all she had to wear for now. So instead he pulled at the ribbon situated at the center of the low neckline, then pushed the fabric off her shoulders and down, until the two firm peaks of flesh were freed.

His chest tightened at the sight of her lily-white skin crowned with the dark blush of her pointed nipples. He closed his hands around the outer curves, pushing slightly inward, and wasted no time bending to lick and suckle.

"Oh Ares," she purred. "Oh Ares—yes, yes." She squirmed beneath him, appearing so shocked at the pleasure that she didn't quite know how to handle it, but he stopped her by propping a thigh securely between hers, using it to pin her to the bed as his aching cock pressed hard against the curve of her hip.

Sucking first one hard bud, then the other, Garon could have sworn her nipples were growing longer and stiffer beneath his ministrations. He moved back and forth, unable to get enough of the rosy beads against his tongue, deep in his mouth, letting her hot moans fuel him. *The first. I am the first to taste of this bounty.*

I am, for her, the first everything!

The thought was so powerful that he couldn't resist

suckling harder, harder, and rubbing his thigh against her pussy, warm even through the leather of his pants and the silk of her dress. The rhythmic moves thrust his swollen cock against her thigh, and soon he was driven to show her just how well her breasts and his shaft could fit together.

Releasing her from his mouth, he moved higher up her body until his stiffened rod dropped into the valley her lush mounds created. He pushed them tight together, folding them fully around his erection as they both basked in the pure pleasure of it. Her moans increased as her small hands curled around the leather that still covered his ass as if to draw him down closer against her.

To his great delight, she flicked the tip of her tongue over the gathering moisture on the end of his shaft, and the wetness she left made for an easy glide when he began to thrust, slow and firm, between her big, lovely breasts.

She looked on the verge of orgasm again already. "I didn't know," she breathed, "about this part."

He couldn't suppress a deep chuckle. "There are *many* possibilities in sex, princess. We invent it all as we go along."

As he fucked her breasts, she lifted them toward him, sighing her rapture. "I like *this* possibility."

Molding and thrusting, he pleased her that way until he realized he needed more. He needed what had made him brave enough to bargain with her, to make her his slave. He needed to sink his cock into her where she was the softest, the warmest, the wettest.

Slowly, he pulled back to kneel between her thighs. She looked beautiful, half dressed, the tumbles of green silk pooling around her supple body, and she became more lovely to him still when he parted her thighs and looked back to her open pussy. She was breathing audibly when he leaned over to drop a quick kiss there, on the visible pink folds.

"Oh…" she gasped, eyes wide with wonder. And then she bit her lip, curiosity shining in her luminous eyes. "What now?"

"Now," he said, the darkness casting a shadow over them both as one candle burned out, "I'm going to take your bride price, princess. I'm going to make you mine once and for all."

CHAPTER FOUR

WHEN HE PLUNGED into her, it was like being pierced by a sword and she screamed at the pain. What had happened? What was wrong? How could this feel so hideous?

She lay beneath him, unable to stop tears from leaking out.

He went still, sighing, and said, "I'm sorry, princess. It's been a long time since I took a virgin. I know it hurts."

This wasn't at all what she'd expected. "I thought sex was…pleasurable."

"It will be," he promised, then lowered a soft kiss to her lips. "Just try to relax your muscles and remember that you want me there, that you want my cock in your sweet little cunt."

Again, she nodded, and tried to do what he said.

And then, in an odd burst of satisfaction and joy, it hit her—he was inside her. Their bodies were joined; she was no longer a virgin. She smiled up at him through the dulling pain.

He grinned back, looking surprised, as he used one thumb to smudge away a tear. "Why are you smiling?"

"You're inside me," she said. "Your cock is inside me. It's…amazing."

He gave her one of his soft, easy grins. "Does it feel better?"

She still felt as if she'd been split apart by something too enormous for the space, but indeed, the pain had faded. "Yes. It's all right now."

"Well, now it will be *more* than all right," he said in an utterly seductive voice that set her heart spinning— and he slowly began to move, to rock to and fro, the motion shifting his cock ever so softly against the inside of her, until she realized that…yes, it was starting to be pleasurable. "How's that?" he whispered.

"More," she whimpered. "I want more."

At that, his moves became more pronounced—he drew slowly out of her, then eased back in. Again. And again. Until she was breathing with him that way, in rhythm with his slow thrusts. And looking into his eyes, whispering, "More, Garon. More."

His strokes came slightly harder and faster, jolting her body, silently urging her to meet them with drives of her own. Soon, she was letting out a little cry of joy at each and so was he, and she *felt* the glorious loss of her virginity, *felt* herself being truly and wholly fucked by a man—the *right* man to take that part of her and make her a woman.

So she was stunned when, without warning, he eased his shaft from her body and rolled behind her in the bed.

She moaned her frustration. "What are you doing? Why did you stop?"

His voice came low, seductive. "I want to do it like this now, princess—want to make you feel my cock even deeper."

"Oh." That was all she needed to hear to be open-minded about the change, still fascinated—not only by the growing pleasure, but by the notion of her body being breached by his, entered by him. It seemed impossibly wonderful.

She let out a quick yelp when he penetrated her from behind, both of them lying on their sides, but the new shot of discomfort subsided almost immediately as he began driving his big, hard tool into her, making her forget pain even existed.

She learned to meet his hard thrusts this way, too, and he was right—she could feel him deeper, and she couldn't help crying out her delight at each and every hot stroke.

Soon enough, though, his moves slowed...into something surprisingly softer, a gentle sort of fucking that seemed to soothe her weariness and all the new worries inside her. He reached around from behind to caress her breast as he kissed her shoulder, then softly brushed his hand back over the hair pulled so tight against her head.

"Take my hair down," she whispered.

"What?"

"Unbind my hair. I'm a virgin no more."

She sensed a short hitch in his rhythm before he resumed sliding into her warmth. "Maybe we shouldn't put that information on display."

She shook her head in front of him, desperately wanting the braid gone and knowing it was right, in every way. "Actually, it will make me less recognizable. And I *need* for it to be down now. I need to be made a woman—like this."

He didn't answer and she didn't know if he was going to comply with her request—until she felt him begin to work at the bands that held her hair.

He continued to move inside her—slow, deep drives of his cock that echoed in the gradual way he parted one lock of hair from the others, untwisting, spreading its fullness across her bare back so that she could feel it beginning to wrap around her, a mane of womanhood, as he stroked into her—deep, deep, deep—below.

She closed her eyes, emotions pummeling her—too many to sort out. All she knew was that she liked where she was and what she was experiencing. She didn't care that she'd promised herself to him as a slave. She didn't care that she'd left her family without a word. She didn't care that she'd left her father without a bride to give for protection of the mountain passes. She didn't care about anything but the masculine hands in her hair and the thick, hard flesh that pulsed inside her now.

Finally, he drew out again, rolling her to her back once more, reaching to draw rippling brown tresses over each of her shoulders down onto her breasts until only the nipples peeked through. "Don't worry—you're undoubtedly a woman now, princess," he said, his eyes glimmering with familiar heat. "You're *all* woman."

With that, he rose to his knees, upright, lifted her thighs to lie atop his, and thrust his cock back between her legs—and this time it came without pain. This time she took it without anything but a gasp of joy as he sank wonderfully deep.

He watched where their bodies met and the mere knowledge of that excited her.

And then he reached down, rubbing his fingers in hot, fast circles over her clit. "Oh!" she moaned as the pleasure hit her hard, thick, rolling through her like something slow and crushing. She met his thrusts and she met his touch, lifting to it, lifting, then closed her eyes, lost to it now, lost to sensation, perspiration, the musky scent of him, the fullness of having him inside her and that delectable stimulation at the top of her slit.

"Come for me," he said, his voice suddenly dark and demanding. Just like when he'd made her his slave. "Come for me *now*."

What I say, you do. His earlier words rushed over her on the heels of the command—and so she came. Hard, her heart threatening to burst from her chest, her pussy throbbing forcefully as the pure delight of sex roared through her, unstoppable. She screamed at each pulse, with no thought of anyone hearing, no thought that anyone in the world existed but the two of them.

"Ah Ares," he bit off just as she was easing down from it, and his thrusts transformed into lunges—hot, powerful lunges that might have hurt if she hadn't welcomed them so much, wanting all her man had to give her. "I'm coming!" he yelled. "I'm coming in you!" And then Laela knew a whole *new* kind of joy, that of taking him to the same place he'd just delivered her.

With a mighty sigh, he slumped down on her, chest to chest. On impulse, she lifted a kiss to his stubbled cheek, even as she sensed him falling into sleep, that quickly.

Thank you, she thought, looking at him. *Thank you for saving me.* He might have made her a slave, but she also felt he'd saved her very life tonight, in more ways than she could even yet comprehend.

WHEN THE SUNLIGHT glancing through the crack in the closed shutters woke Laela the next morning, she lay alone in the bed. All evidence of what had happened the night before remained—her dress lying unkempt around her waist, the bindings from her braid strewn on the fur bed covering—but her lover was gone and a feeling of uneasiness had taken his place.

Slowly, she adjusted her dress, covering her nakedness, and went to the small wash basin against one wall, splashing a bit of cool water on her face. She glanced about for a viewing glass, anxious to see herself with her hair falling free around her shoulders. But when she didn't find one anywhere in the room, she remembered that such luxuries were not nearly so common beyond the walls of a lavish fortress. Of course, she'd seen herself with her hair down before, but just never outside her bedchamber, never out in the world where the loose locks truly signified something.

Making her way gingerly to the door, she eased it open to find the outer tavern room in total disarray from the previous night, the tables scattered with half-empty goblets and covered with spilled ale, not yet dried. Ares, what a mess!

When the outer door suddenly burst open, both Garon and Baelor walked in, laughing. Baelor ate a slice of fruit bread so fresh she could smell the fruits and spices from across the room. Garon toted a small cloth bag in one hand.

"Glad to see you're awake," he said matter-of-factly as his gaze pinned her in place, just as sexual as the night before. Her pussy spasmed softly beneath her dress, just from that. "I've brought a fresh loaf of bread for breakfast, but you'll have to eat while you work. First you'll clear and wash the goblets, then you'll need to scrub the tables and sweep the floor."

She blinked. "Me?" So much for sex and spasms.

He lowered his chin as if to chide her. "This place won't clean itself, princess. And we have an arrangement, if you recall."

She drew in her breath and tried to look tougher than she felt at the moment. He might call her a princess, yet just now she felt like anything but. "Yes, of course. I just thought the other two women…"

He and Baelor exchanged light grins. "They are both sleeping off a very long night in Baelor's bed up the way." He pointed vaguely northward. "Since *you're* here, there's no need to disturb them, and it will save me what I would normally pay them to do the job."

She forced an awkward nod. *You agreed to this. What he says, you do. You're not a little girl anymore, nor a royal daughter.* "Of course."

Seeming pleased by her simple reply, Garon reached in his sack and drew out a steaming hot loaf, the same fruit bread Baelor ate, and passed it into her arms. "Knives are in that cabinet," he said, pointing toward the corner of the room. "Slice up our breakfast."

Laela felt a bit wooden as she found a blade and proceeded to cut crooked pieces of bread. She'd never performed such a task before—up to now, everything had always been done *for* her. And it wasn't that Garon was being *cold* to her exactly, but certainly one would never guess the two of them had shared such intimacies the previous night. She'd imagined a much…*warmer* reception when she'd departed the bedroom looking for him, and she couldn't quell the disappointment flowing through her.

A few minutes later, she served the bread with goblets of water on a wooden platter. Garon picked up the first slice of bread, examining it closely, then glanced at Baelor before looking back to her, his eyes tinged with amusement. "Your first time in a kitchen, I presume."

She nodded.

"You'll get better at it. Now eat and get to work."

She drew in her breath at the command, growing more miffed by the second, but then she remembered the alternative—doing with the old man Ogran what she'd done last night with Garon. To avoid *that* fate, she would happily clean the tavern from top to bottom and put up with a bit of gruffness, as well.

"The new look of your hair becomes you," Baelor said.

She turned to find the young man wearing a knowing grin, a grin which reminded her that out here, outside the fortress, sex was commonplace, nothing secretive. It didn't matter that what she'd shared with Garon had felt profound and moving to her—out here, everyone had sex with everyone else. So she couldn't blush or act shy. Instead, she summoned a smile and tried her best to look alluring. "I…enjoyed letting Garon take it down for me."

"So I heard."

And to Laela's surprise, the very act of acknowledging sex with Garon to his friend made her feel…provocative, both excited and exciting. The earlier tingling sensation between her legs returned, soft but potent, and her nipples tightened under the silk.

She flashed a look at her lover, her…master, she supposed, imagining him sharing the details of their bedplay with Baelor. Yesterday, the notion would have embarrassed her, but today…well, today, everything was different. Envisioning the two men discussing her body and what Garon had done with her only intensified the flow of heat that currently rushed through her nether regions.

Out here, sex was simply…sex. She might *want* it to be more, but that was one more luxury she didn't possess, and she'd have to get used to doing without *any* luxuries from this point forward. In the meantime, she'd just gained a new, rather delicious understanding of how to…well, how to *appreciate* it for what it was. For with even this most subtle of discussions about it, the air in the room had grown hotter, along with Laela's cunt. Obviously, *everything* about sex with Garon thrilled her—even having him share it with his friend.

Such sensual amusement laced Garon's gaze that she almost wondered if he could read her mind. "Get to work and be a good little tavern maid today," he said, "and maybe tonight I'll give you some new things to enjoy."

IT WAS PERHAPS the longest day of Laela's life. She'd had no notion of how hard the maids in the fortress worked to keep things in order. And her work, it turned out, wasn't done when the outer room was clean and ready to open again for business that night. The moment she finished *that* work, Garon instructed her to tidy up the bedroom, as well, and then to wash the rags and drying cloths used the previous night in the tavern in a big wooden tub behind the building.

It was nearly nightfall when she emptied the dirty water and stepped back inside. Garon sat in a chair at one of the long tables, his feet propped atop it. He'd already lit thick candles to illuminate the tavern for the evening and, in the dim glow, his eyes glittered with open sensuality.

"How was your day, princess?" He used the words, accompanied by a smile, to tease her. She'd made the mistake of thinking he wasn't arrogant, but he *was*—about some things. About his control over her, definitely.

"Tiring, but fine."

He looked impressed by her fortitude, tipping his head back slightly. "Well, Sima and Janya will be here soon to serve the ale and entertain the customers. You should get some rest." He hiked a thumb toward the bedroom.

Thankful for the respite, she nodded.

Then another wicked grin spread across his handsome face. "Don't sleep *too* deeply, though, princess. I'll be waking you later to entertain *me*."

Despite her weariness, Laela let that promise fuel her and discovered she was not too exhausted to wish for more sex with him. She even managed a small smile, replying, "I shall let anticipation give me sweet dreams." She departed the room reveling in the sensations that took hold of her body when Garon looked at her with hungry eyes.

Garon watched her go, her green skirt fluttering with the sway of her pretty ass as she left the tavern room. She'd surprised him, working so hard with never a complaint. It at once raised his opinion of her and irritated him. For had she complained, he could have grown angry with her, thought her a spoiled little royal not worthy of his concern. He could have cancelled their agreement and thrown her out. As it was, it only added to his growing respect for the girl.

All the more reason to remember she's your slave and treat her that way.

He couldn't soften toward her—it was bad enough he was letting her stay. But so long as he kept his distance—emotionally—no problems would arise. A sensible man simply didn't start caring for his ruler's runaway daughter—only madness and regret could come of it.

Damnation, a sensible man didn't let himself care for *any* woman. The first—and last—woman he'd cared for had run away with another man, a man who could give her finer dresses and a better home than he could. Now, he possessed much more than he'd had then, but still preferred living simply, spending his earnings only on things he needed.

He'd learned his lesson when his former lover had left him, learned there was no gain to be had from putting trust in a female, letting himself love someone—and the fact that Laela was on the run from Enrick, Ruler of Caralon, only made her that much more forbidden.

Of course, he'd already dipped into that forbidden nectar last night—and what a sweet, hot dip it had been. But sex—and work—was *all* he planned to take from her.

And as for tonight's taking, he had special plans for the girl. Plans that would remind both of them that she was his sex slave, and that he was her master.

He glanced toward the door she'd just disappeared through. *Rest well, princess, for last night was gentle, but tonight you will know what it is to truly be a man's plaything.*

THE CREAK OF the bedroom door jarred Laela from sleep. All was dark, even outside the room, the tavern quiet and still. Nearby, the flame of a candle flickered to life until she saw her lover gazing down on her, his face in shadow. He had come for her. And she was so very ready. Just as she had predicted, she had dreamed of him, dreamed of his touches, of his kisses, and now she wanted even more of him than her dreams had supplied.

But when a bit of movement across the room drew her eye back to the door, she glanced over to find Baelor stepping inside, as well. Still in a state of half sleep, she struggled desperately to wrap her mind around the situation as Garon sat down on the bed next to her, splaying his large hand across her stomach.

She looked up at him, bold arousal flaring through her from the touch, his palm warm through the thin silk.

As he bent to kiss her, long, deep, his tongue mingling with hers, he slid his hand up the fabric of her dress to close over her breast. The caress made her sigh, sensation trickling from her chest all the way down to her pussy, which had been aching for him, despite her weariness. And the heat somehow deepened even more when she again caught sight of dark-haired Baelor lowering himself into a simple wooden chair near the door.

Even so, she closed her hands around Garon's forearms, pushing him back lightly. "Why is...why is Baelor here?"

Garon's gaze turned hard on her, possessive. "You are my slave, remember?"

Despite the long day of work just past, the darkness of his voice, his words, dug deep inside her, touching her intimately. She nodded.

"You do what I say. Don't you recall agreeing to that?"

"Yes, of course, and willingly. But why is...what is...?" She looked back to Baelor, whose eyes shone glassy with lust as Garon pulled her dress off one shoulder, revealing one plump breast, the nipple pink and erect. More unbidden excitement shuddered through her at knowing Baelor saw, yet still she looked back to Garon, seeking to understand.

"Tonight, princess," he said, his gaze narrowing darkly on her, "Baelor is going to watch."

She couldn't hide her astonishment. "Watch?"

Garon's voice went colder, harder, than she'd heard

it before. "Do you dare protest?"

She let out a breath of pure confusion. "No, I just…didn't know. Men can take pleasure in just…watching?"

He tilted his head, clearly reminded of just how ignorant she was in the ways of sex. "Of course."

He'd said it matter-of-factly, as if it were obvious. It made her recall how all the tavern's patrons had watched Sima and Janya kissing and touching last night, and the memory forced her to revisit her *own* reluctant response to their show as well. "I…just didn't know. I'm sorry."

Garon looked almost regretful that he'd responded so gruffly, perhaps realizing now that she'd not meant to argue, only to grasp what was happening. He lifted a gentle hand to her cheek. "It's all right, princess." Then he pushed her dress from her other shoulder and said, "Take this off. Let us show Baelor your lovely nude cunt."

She should have resented Garon for this—but strangely, instead she found herself wanting nothing more than to please him. And if pleasing him meant pleasing Baelor…well, Baelor was not an unattractive man, so if she was honest with herself, it was not a task she found distasteful. She also probably should have been terrified—but she didn't suffer that emotion, either. As both men's lustful eyes drank in her curves, what she felt leaned much closer to pure excitement, anticipation, and as she flicked her gaze from Garon to his friend, her nipples puckered tighter and her pussy wept with desire.

Sitting up in the bed, Laela slowly eased the dress down around her waist, over the arc of her hips, finally pushing it to her ankles. And with each inch of skin she revealed, it felt somehow as if a bright light were being shone upon it, upon everything sexual inside her that remained so eager to be released. The air in the room felt still, heavy, and her every limb seemed filled with hot, tense energy as she waited to see what came next.

"Spread your legs for him," Garon said.

She met his eyes, and the hot glimmer in them fueled her further. Parting her thighs wide across the fur bed covering, she leaned back on her elbows, letting both men look their fill. She feared she might melt from the pure pleasure it brought her.

"Ah—as beautiful as you said," Baelor murmured, and it was clear from his awestruck eyes that he'd never seen a denuded pussy before, either. Both men's gazes burned into her, making her wetter, so wet that she wondered... "Can you see how damp your eyes make me?" she asked softly.

Garon's slow grin was laced with fire. "Yes, princess. Your cunt shimmers in the candlelight."

"Like a handful of tiny gems," Baelor added with an equally lascivious smile.

Their lusty expressions—all for her, for her body—made her want...she wasn't even sure *what* exactly she yearned for, only that it was new. She'd thought Garon had turned her into a wholly sexual being last night, but tonight the tension was ratcheted still higher, making her pussy tingle and her breasts ache with such unadulterated longing that, in that moment, she thought she would happily do *anything*, anything he wanted, anything he asked. Which was good, she reminded herself—for she was his slave and had promised exactly that.

"The only way your pussy could look more lovely, Laela, is with my cock in it," Garon said, eyes still aglitter.

She went breathless with how badly she suddenly craved just that. "Mmm…yes," was all she could get out.

She watched with bated breath as Garon shed his leather vest, then worked at the lacings of his dark brown pants until his shaft popped free. She licked her lips, the sight taking her back to last night. She had at first been dumbfounded at the size of it—it must be eight or nine inches in length—and was sure it would never fit inside her. Later, though, after that nasty bit of pain, she discovered how wrong she'd been and how gloriously such a cock melded with her cunt. Tonight, the initial sight of the hard column of flesh was just as shocking— yet at the same time it made her pussy pulse with unbridled hunger. "Fuck me," she whispered in the soft candlelight.

She heard Baelor sigh in awe at the request, but kept her gaze on Garon, whose wicked smile said he would do as she asked, even as he teased her. "You forget your place, princess. Who is the slave here?"

She returned a playful grin. "I am."

"And who is the master?"

"You are. Master." Then she lowered her chin, casting a naughty, daring look. "Now fuck me, master."

Appearing just as entranced as *she* felt, Garon crawled toward her from the foot of the bed, same as last night, except tonight he was naked, the muscles in his shoulders shifting smoothly beneath his skin, his majestic cock arcing upward on his belly—*and* they had an audience. And still, Baelor's presence heightened her desire for her lover rather than hampered it. On impulse, she sent the dark-haired man a quick glance to let him know she didn't mind his being there.

Tonight, as he positioned his body over hers, Garon did not plunge his cock into her, but gently pushed, prodded. As her cunt remained tight and a bit sore, she appreciated his lenience and tried to help by meeting the small, light thrusts. Despite last night's pain, that part of her body yearned for him, perhaps even more now that she knew the wonder of having him deep inside her. "I want you in me," she purred hotly, lifting her hips from the fur beneath to meet him.

"And you will have me," he promised, leaning forward to close his hands over the globes of her breasts.

He kneaded them like the maids at home kneaded dough for bread, his rough fingers pressing deep and thorough into her flesh, sending tendrils of hot pleasure all through her and making her pussy wetter, wetter…until finally his cock began to ease its way inside. They both moaned as it slid deeper on a moist path of heat.

"Oh Garon," she breathed, pulling him to her, wrapping her arms around his broad shoulders as much as she could. She needed him near her, this man who had saved her from imminent peril, this man who had shown her—and was *still* showing her—the marvelous joys of sex.

He moved in her slowly, hotly, both of them sighing their pleasure as they found a grinding rhythm that seemed to lead them both toward ecstasy. Their eyes met, connecting them in yet another way as his tremendous shaft plowed deeper, deeper into her softness below. "You fill me," she whispered up to him, voice labored with passion.

"Your pussy is so tight around my cock, princess. So good, so tight."

She liked the low murmur, the heavy-lidded look of his eyes—liked knowing that she, an inexperienced royal girl, was able to push a man like Garon so far into passion.

Gradually, his thrusts grew harder, faster. And as good as the slow, deep strokes had felt to her, she enjoyed the change, relishing the power emanating from his muscular body, from his long, hard cock. She felt possessed by him, each hot stroke pounding through her very being, the sensations echoing all the way out to her fingers and toes. She yelled out her joy at each.

He thrust faster, even faster—and so gloriously hard—each lunge driving impossibly deep into her welcoming cunt, until something inside Laela began to turn wild, almost crazy, out of control. In one sense, the pleasure was too great, but in another, she hungered for more of it. She could scarcely understand the recklessness tearing through her as she began to writhe beneath him, in one second gripping tight into the fur at her sides, in the next, beating the bed with her fists—wild, depraved, desperate and filled with indecipherable longing. "Oh, I want more of you. More of you!"

Above her, Garon gave a dirty little laugh and said, "What more of me is there to have, princess? I'm already giving you every inch of the hot, hard cock you crave so much." As if to remind her, he concluded with a particularly jarring stroke that shook her to her core.

Yet still a confusing frustration ruled her as she rolled and twisted beneath him. "I don't know, I just wish…I wish I could have your cock between my breasts, like last night. Oh, and in my mouth, too! But I love it filling my pussy, as well. I want to have it *everywhere*. Everywhere, all at once." With that, she let her eyes fall shut, lifting her hips even higher, trying to swallow his shaft somehow deeper between her thighs. She simply wanted more. More sensation, everywhere.

When she wrenched her eyes back open, she found her lover looking slowly over to Baelor, then back to her. Oh Ares—she'd nearly forgotten the other man was even there!

Garon's gaze narrowed and all amusement left his voice. "If you're so hungry for a cock in your mouth, princess, perhaps Baelor would be willing to provide one."

Laela sucked in her breath at the suggestion, shocked. But almost as quickly, she grew rather…intrigued by the notion. Intrigued—and aroused. She'd forgotten Baelor was there, but now that she remembered, her skin prickled, wondering about the possibilities. She was nearly breathless when she spoke. "Is…is this…possible? For a woman to be with…more than one man at the same time?"

Low, masculine laughter filled the room around her before Baelor answered. "I was with both Sima and Janya just last night—why did you think they were sleeping in my bed?"

"I don't know," she mumbled, feeling sheepish.

"In sex, princess," Garon said, taking on the voice of an educator, "the possibilities are limitless—just as I told you last night." Then he looked to Baelor. "Come join us, my friend. Come help me give our little Laela what she yearns for."

CHAPTER FIVE

L AELA TRIED TO catch her breath as Baelor moved to the bed. She wanted this—the roiling lust low in her belly told her she did—but she wasn't sure she was ready for it. Dear Ares, she'd just lost her virginity last night! And now, two men—and two big, hard, glorious cocks—at once?

Garon's strong hand molded to her shoulder, drawing her gaze back to him. "Relax, princess," he whispered, his voice barely audible, his expression comforting. "The pleasure only multiplies from here."

Taking a place with them on the bed, Baelor stripped off his tunic to reveal a chest lightly corded with muscle, but not as broad or tan as Garon's. Next, he reached for the lacings on his pants. Laela watched, curious, still not quite able to believe she was about to get acquainted with a second man's shaft so quickly. Part of her felt horribly wicked, but another part of her relished this opportunity, something she'd never even dreamed of and now would experience to the fullest.

As Baelor pushed down black leather pants, his cock burst forth, looking hard and red and ready, and although not as large as Garon's, it was still undeniably attractive. Shoving the pants off completely, he rose to his knees at Laela's side.

Biting her lip speculatively, she lifted her gaze from this new specimen to Garon's face. "Touch it, princess," he urged, even as he continued to move inside her, sliding his cock in and out of her cunt in smooth, wet strokes.

Taking a deep breath, still potently aware of the erection inside her, she gingerly reached out to close her fist around Baelor's shaft. Warm to the touch, it flinched lightly in her grasp as he let out a soft moan that fueled her desire to have both of them at once.

She squeezed gently, beginning to work the hard column of flesh in a rhythm to match the other rod's strokes inside her. So hard in her hand. So hard in her pussy. Thrilled, she met Baelor's gaze, then Garon's.

"Would you like it in your mouth, or between your breasts?" Garon asked.

A difficult decision—both suggestions made her body burn hotter still. "My mouth," she finally said, and so ready that her skin itched with wanting it, she boldly drew his cock toward her lips.

Baelor balanced on his knees next to her turned head as she raked a thorough lick over the end of his erection. She tasted the fluid gathered there, something she'd noticed on Garon's cock last night, as well. "What *is* that?" she asked both men, licking at it again. "What is the wetness that gathers here at the tip?"

Garon replied. "It's what shoots from our cocks when we come, princess." His slight smile reminded her of her ignorance, but she sensed he was growing used to it now and maybe even starting to like it a little. "There will much more of it then, though."

She nodded, ready to sink into her new pleasure, and lowered her mouth over the head of Baelor's rod. She felt his hot groan between her thighs, where Garon still dealt out a firm, steady fuck, and it fueled her further, deeper onto the shaft between her lips. Soon enough she was suckling him as she had Garon last night, timing it with Garon's strokes.

As Baelor's hand curled warmly around one of her breasts, squeezing, molding, Garon began to stroke his thumb over her clit, just above the point where their bodies met. Pure pleasure enveloped Laela—pleasure like nothing she'd ever known or could even have imagined. She was a girl no longer. No, she was a grown woman taking two delectable shafts into her body while her men touched and caressed her where she needed it most. She moaned around Baelor's cock, driven to take him as deeply as she could, all the way to her throat, as Garon's strokes dug deeper and harder, finding her very core. Both men thrust at her, and she welcomed it with all that she was, letting herself get lost in the tumult of sensation. She sensed the motions of their cocks everywhere, not merely in pussy and mouth, but low in her belly, outward to her fingers and toes, vibrating through her with a power unlike any she'd ever experienced.

So when Garon pulled out of her, she went still, stunned—feeling abandoned.

She flashed him a look of disbelief, even as her lips remained wrapped around Baelor's cock, and he let out a chuckle. "Don't be angry, princess. There's more to come."

She let Baelor slip from her mouth. "There had *better* be."

Both men laughed and only then did she realize how hungry and demanding she had become. Garon brought his face down near hers to speak low in her ear. "I'm glad you like Baelor's cock so much, because he is like a brother to me. And brothers share many things, Laela. Now, I'm going to share your pussy with him, let him fuck you hard and deep."

Her heart beat mercilessly in her chest and the truth was, in that moment, as long as *someone* fucked her, she hardly cared who. So long as she had a long, hard shaft inside her—and, well, as long as Garon desired it for her. For she wanted what *he* wanted, wanted to please him more than she could easily understand. "And what will *you* do to me, master?"

He tilted his head with a brazen smile. "Well, my little sex slave, I'm going to give you something I already know you like. I'm going to slide my cock between your lovely breasts."

"Mmm," she purred, anticipating the sheer joy of it.

"And they're going to be slick with your own juices, princess, wet with the moisture from deep in your tight little cunt."

Again she sighed, aroused by all that was happening—every promise, and the anticipation of having them kept.

She didn't have to wait, for Garon quickly straddled her waist, letting his shaft drop between her breasts. She eyed it hungrily as he pressed the mounds of flesh up around it, enclosing it completely. "Oh…" she moaned, and just then, although she couldn't see past Garon's towering form, Baelor pushed his cock into her below. "Oh Ares!"

Within another few seconds, she was again lost to the depths of delight, her body nothing but a sexual tool. She wanted nothing more in that moment than to keep fucking both men forever.

As Garon thrust between her breasts, she opened her mouth, letting him know she would welcome his cock there, as well. So he slid deeper, longer, until the head of his marvelous shaft slipped between her lips at each stroke. She tasted herself, smelled her juices on them both, met Baelor's thrusts, and simply basked in the hot joy of it for seconds, minutes, hours—she didn't know how long, but she simply let it consume her.

Behind closed eyes, she let herself sink into the notion of two strong, lovely men riding her, the vision the three of them must create together. What would they look like if someone peered through a crack in the closed shutters into the candlelit room? She went even wetter at the idea. Mmm, yes, more evidence that much pleasure could be taken just from watching. Although Baelor was doing far more than watching *now*.

Finally Garon moved off of her, lowering a warm kiss to her lips even as Baelor still thrust inside her below. "Let her ride you, Baelor," he instructed.

Baelor didn't hesitate, extracting his cock to leave her feeling suddenly, shockingly…empty. Again, though, Garon reassured her with a chuckle. "Don't panic, princess. You will like this even better."

Her breath still came heavy, labored, as she stared up in silence, waiting to see if this particular promise was true. Baelor shifted to his back, his slick shaft angling upward.

"Climb on," Garon urged.

"Onto his…?"

He grinned. "Yes, onto his cock. You will feel it even deeper, and there will be other delights involved, as well."

Slowly, Laela did something she was starting to get rather good at, she thought—following Garon's orders. But thus far, other than a bit of physical labor, the man had brought her nothing but pleasure…and safety…so there was no reason to even think of resisting.

As she impaled herself on Baelor's still-rigid cock, she let out a sigh—Ares, she *could* feel it deeper. Incredibly so. She looked to Garon, wondering what his even *bigger* rod would feel like in this position.

"Now move on him," Garon said. She hesitated slightly, feeling a bit lost, until Garon added with a grin, "They say riding a cock is something like riding a horse—although I've never ridden either myself."

Laela thought of the few times she'd ridden the horses in her father's stables. Teesia was far more interested in the activity, so Laela suspected this skill had probably come much more naturally to her sister than it would to her—yet the moment she pushed her pussy against Baelor, then eased back, then bore down slightly again, she understood the pleasure to be found here. It left her in a soft, hot moan, the sensation echoing through her whole body.

"Mmm, yes," she purred softly, ever so aware of Garon's eyes riveted on her, and letting his gaze fuel her desire even more. She cast him a coquettish look, daring to softly say, "When I press against him, it rubs my clit."

His grin widened, going wicked. "Indeed it does. And I'm discovering I very much like to watch you take your pleasure, princess. So ride him. Ride that hard cock that's stretching so far up inside you. Take your pleasure from it, Laela. And I'll take mine, too."

As she moved more boldly against Baelor, her hips easing into a natural grinding motion, Garon situated himself behind her, his chest to her back, his cock to her ass, his arms closing warmly around her waist from behind. "Mmm," she moaned, amazed once again at the joys of feeling two men against her.

It was as Garon's large hands closed around her

breasts, squeezing, caressing, that his enormous cock slid neatly into place in the valley of her ass. She couldn't have anticipated how good it would feel, wedged there against her, and when he bent to kiss her neck, she turned to meet his mouth with hers.

His tongue mingled with her own as her body seemed to take flight from every thrilling touch and connection with both men. "This is…unbelievable," she managed with labored breaths between kisses.

Garon nipped sensuously at her lower lip, then smiled into her eyes. "*You* are unbelievable."

Her movements became more pronounced—adding stimulation both in front, at her clit, and in back, too. She still couldn't fathom why or how Garon's erection felt so wonderful pressed against her there, especially when—oh Ares—when he seemed to begin nudging the hard tip at her. "What are you doing?" she asked over her shoulder, breathless. "That feels so incredible."

"Ares," Baelor said on a hot sigh below her. "Are you going to fuck her ass while I'm in her pussy?"

The three maintained the same rhythm, never letting it waver, Laela's breasts bouncing in Garon's strong hands as her nether regions soaked up delights from every direction. "No," Garon replied, sounding breathless. "Not now. She's not ready for that yet." He pulled her hair aside to nibble at her neck again. "But sometime maybe. Sometime later. Sometime…definitely," he added with a deep, hearty laugh.

Fuck her *ass*? He could do *that*? *There*?

Part of her wanted to ask, to learn—but the rest of her was too swept away by what was *already* happening to her. Sensation *everywhere*. But most notably at the front and rear of her cunt. Each grinding move carried her back and forth, back and forth, between the two exquisite pressures. She began to wish Garon *would* fuck her ass, even without quite understanding how such a thing could work. She only knew his cock felt magnificent there, pushing her closer and closer to that hot peak of joy—and that fucking Baelor, rubbing against him again and again, took her over...the...edge.

"Oh! Oh Ares! Oh Ares! Oh yes, Ares, yes!"

She cried out through the entire orgasm, utterly amazed at the power, the driving force of it. It seemed to go on and on, echoing through her like relentless thunder—until Baelor groaned and said, "Ares, I'm coming, too," then smoothly lifted her off him to shoot hot white fluid onto her belly.

As the two panted and sighed, coming down from the pleasure, Garon's arms latched tight around her waist to begin rubbing the wetness vigorously into her skin, the very act exciting her all over again, that quickly. She sighed at the dark arousal, luxuriating in it as the liquid warmed her—then yelped, surprised, when Garon suddenly flipped her to her back on the bed and rammed his own hard rod inside her. "Oh!" she sobbed at the shocking delight, immediately reminded that he was bigger than his friend.

Thrust, thrust, thrust—each came rough and demanding, but she met them fiercely, feeling as wild as *he* suddenly seemed. "Ah Ares," he moaned, and Laela knew instinctively that he was coming now, too. She lay beneath him, legs spread as wide as possible for him as he spilled his seed inside her.

When he finally went still, quiet, collapsing gently atop her, she thought of having had both Garon and Baelor's lovely cocks inside her pussy—and let out a joyous, trilling laugh.

Garon turned his head to meet her gaze. "Something humorous, princess?"

"I just…never knew I was such a wanton," she admitted.

He grinned. "And now?"

"I *am*. I most certainly and absolutely *am*."

The three chuckled over her revelation, but she noticed now that only Garon touched her—his body wrapped warmly around her, in fact. In the moment she realized the change, Baelor rose on one elbow next to her and said to them both, "I should go. I promised to meet Sima and Janya at my house before…well, before this particular opportunity arose." He leaned in to lower a chaste kiss on Laela's cheek, even as Garon nuzzled the other. "By now, they've probably forgotten me, pleasured each *other* and fallen asleep, but *should* they still be waiting for me, I wouldn't want to deprive them," he concluded with a wink, then eased from the bed to quietly put on his clothes and slip out the door.

Laela had enjoyed Baelor's visit—she'd enjoyed it

more than she could have conceived—yet at the same time, she was glad he was gone, pleased to share the candlelight with Garon alone.

They stayed quiet for a time, Laela reminiscing on all the sensations she'd experienced tonight, and thinking about the two men who had so generously delivered them.

"You said Baelor was like a brother to you," she finally whispered, turning to look at Garon.

His eyes were shut, but he opened them. "Yes."

"How did that come to be?"

He hesitated slightly, looking sleepy, but answered anyway. "We met as boys, right here in the village. It was in the time just before your father came into power, before all the domains of Caralon had been united as one, so there was still war in the region."

She'd learned about those years from Aris in their classes, but this reminded her just how recent such times *were*. Even in the year of her birth, Caralon had remained divided—only shortly after did her father's armies push down the last rogue leaders to make the domain what it was today.

"I'll never forget it," Garon said, his voice suddenly seeming far away. "I was just a child myself when I saw another little boy come wandering into the settlement alone. I lived with my grandfather then, so I went to our hut to find him. Baelor couldn't have been more than three or four years old, and it was difficult to get him to talk, but my grandfather slowly coaxed from him that his parents had been killed in an attack near the northern border of Caralon."

"Virgs?" she asked fearfully. The heathen warriors of Virgland still threatened Caralon's borders on occasion now—Maven's husband Dane had battled them as recently as a few years ago, shortly after their marriage.

He nodded. "Slowly, we figured out that his parents had been farmers, peaceful people, but the Virgs know no peace—only killing and destruction. A caravan of other survivors had brought Baelor south, but turned him out near the village, likely because none had the means to provide for him. My grandfather took him in and though he's seven years younger than me, we were raised as brothers."

"Your grandfather sounds like a kind man." Often in Caralonian society, parentless children were indeed taken in and even treated well by the community—but seldom did one person take sole responsibility for the child of another.

Garon nodded. "My mother died during childbirth, so he raised me."

So much death in the lives of these men. It made her feel fortunate to have both of her parents, even if she *was* still incredibly angry with her father. "You were born here then, in Myrtell?" she asked.

Garon shook his head against the fur bed covering. "My grandfather and my mother—his daughter—both worked as servants in a large fortress far away, somewhere west of here. The man they worked for is my father, although not by my mother's choice. He raped her."

Laela gasped. Rape? It was a crime perpetrated by such as the Virgs, but in Caralon itself, the offense was rare. Except for royal daughters and a few other wealthy girls with a bride price, sex was a common, accepted way to entertain one's self, a celebrated pastime that all shared with equal joy, and she knew, just from her knowledge of their society, that finding a willing partner was not difficult. Rape was an act committed by only the most violent of men.

Garon seemed to read her thoughts. "The fortress was isolated. Not many young women worth fucking, I presume," he said coldly. Yet his voice came steady, and she knew he'd accepted this harsh reality of his life long ago. "After my mother's death, my grandfather stole me away and brought me here. There, I could have been a wealthy landowner with a fortress of my own someday—probably by now—but Ares only knows what sort of existence I'd have had to endure. My grandfather felt a chance at a happy life for me was worth the sacrifice."

She summoned a soft smile. "And *are* you happy?"

He met her gaze in the dim lighting. "Mostly, I suppose. When my grandfather died, he'd saved enough for me to open the tavern. So I have more than many in Myrtell—something to call my own. I have food to eat and ale to drink, and earnings saved should I ever need them. I have a soft bed, and enough women to warm it. *You* to warm it, just now," he added, reaching to press his hand across her bare belly. "And he left me other things, too. Not things that can be measured, but…"

"What?" she asked when he trailed off.

"He taught me things. He gave me an education."

She couldn't help being curious what he meant exactly. "What did he teach you?"

His eyes softened. "He read. And he taught me to read, too."

She smiled at his pride in his grandfather, knowing that, in Caralon, many did not have the opportunity to learn the ancient written language. "My father's fortress possessed a large library stacked to the ceiling with old, valuable volumes from the Before Times."

She rolled on her side to face him. "Really? They must have been extremely valuable."

He nodded. "And yet there they all were, tucked away in a fort in the middle of nowhere, gathering dust. The master of the fortress didn't even read them. As far as my grandfather knew, they were left behind by *his* parents, and only my grandfather ever set foot in the chamber." Then he grinned. "He used to sneak in late every night to read. Read almost the whole library, he said. And he told me stories from the volumes, and taught me everything he could remember learning from them."

It gave her chills to think of such treasures going unappreciated. Enrick, too, owned a library, but even the Ruler of Caralon's collection was small, containing only a few fragile volumes from the Before Times. "*My* father's library," she said, feeling giddy at the sudden memory, "had a favorite volume I learned from as a little girl. It was a book of primeval tales, and my favorite of them featured what, in the Before Times, was called a *kingdom*. The man who ruled it, as my father rules Caralon, was the *king*. He had a daughter—the story was much about her—and she was called a…" She started to say it, but stopped, meeting his gaze.

He smiled, then finished for her. "A princess."

She'd nearly forgotten to wonder how he'd known the archaic term—so much had happened so fast over the past two nights—but now it all came clear. His grandfather *had* taught him a lot. "He sounds," she said, "like a wonderful man. I'm…glad you had someone like that in your life."

"Why is that, princess?"

She spoke quietly, sheepishly—but truthfully. "Because I think he made *you* into a good man, too."

His brows knit doubtfully. "A man who protects you only if you agree to be his slave is a good man?"

She considered his words, and replied honestly. "I'll admit, it doesn't *sound* very good. But so far, yes, I *do* think you're a good man—perhaps a better man than you know."

THE NEXT DAY Garon walked along the beach, listening to the seabirds call, watching the grasses on the dunes sway in the ocean breeze. The hottest days of summer were upon Myrtell, a time that often led him to the shore for that blessed wind that whipped through his hair and took his mind off the heat for a little while.

At the moment, though, he had a much more niggling sort of heat on his mind—and the sea breeze wasn't distracting him from it. He kept remembering Laela so boldly taking both his cock and Baelor's. He'd been sure the very suggestion would send her escaping out the nearest window—yet he'd been wrong. Instead, she'd stunned and amazed him with her lovely willingness. No one would have believed she was a virgin until just a couple of days ago.

Seemed he simply couldn't upset the girl—no matter what intentions he began with early in the evening, by the time the last candle's flame faded, he was forced to realize he'd made her far happier than sad. It had only been two nights, but two very *telling* nights indeed.

He'd known from the moment he'd lain eyes on her that she was a lush beauty whose body could threaten his sanity—but he'd had no way of knowing she'd turn out to be such a hot, willing little slave.

Both nights, he'd come to her intent on ravishing her, making her damnably sorry she'd ever enslaved herself to him, but each night, after finding her so impossibly agreeable to whatever he suggested, he'd soon forgotten all about wanting to offend her, trying to drive her to protest or, better yet, drive her away—he'd been far too caught up in watching her explore the wonders of her own body, and of his. And, last night, Baelor's, too.

And now…now she thought he was a good man?

What had he been thinking, opening up to her about his grandfather? It had been too late in the night for such a discussion—he'd spoken without weighing his words.

The truth was—he didn't think he was a particularly *good* man or a particularly *bad* one. He'd been a *better* man before his grandfather's death, but once the beloved old man had passed on, Garon had been left with no one to care about anymore. Oh, there was Baelor, certainly, but that was different. Maybe the loss of his grandfather had left him feeling as if…well, as if no one *needed* him anymore.

And then he'd fallen for Ellaena, who'd left him for a wealthier man, and for a brief measure of time Garon had even wished his grandfather *hadn't* taken him away from the riches that would have been his, for riches bought a lot in this world—maybe even love. He'd come to his senses later, realizing he remained glad his grandfather had not let him be raised by a rapist—but life had indeed changed after those losses, his grandfather and Ellaena. Life had become about serving ale and fucking women. Nothing wrong with either activity, but he couldn't deny his existence had begun to feel…thin. He'd slowly grown greedy, selfish, out for himself.

The man who'd agreed to protect Laela when she'd come to him, fear and desperation in her eyes—*that* was the man his grandfather had raised. But the man who'd made her promise her body for it, the man who'd made her a slave, was someone his grandfather wouldn't be so proud of.

Yet what it came down to was simple—he couldn't permit her to see what was left of the good man inside him from this point forward.

Because he couldn't harbor this royal girl much longer.

He was only lucky Enrick's men hadn't yet returned to haul them both away, him to his death.

She was sweet—too sweet for him to throw her out into the street, he'd learned. So it had to be *her* decision—she had to decide to go on her own. Which meant he'd have to make life as his sex slave unbearable. He'd have to insist she indulge in acts that she would find repulsive, and he'd have to *succeed* in finding those repulsive acts, even if that required digging a bit deeper into depravity than he'd gone so far. He'd have to make her decide that marriage to whatever old man her father had chosen for her was better than what she'd be forced to do for *him*, here.

Letting himself play with the girl up to now had been decadent fun, but also pure foolishness. As much as he genuinely liked her, and as much delight as he took from her enthusiasm in the bedroom, his very life depended upon getting her out of his tavern—for good.

LAELA STOOD OVER a wooden tub, methodically scrubbing the goblets dirtied the night before. She should have felt dejected—suddenly living the life of a washerwoman. Yet even without a viewing glass to peer into, she knew a merry little smile lit her face. For every time she recalled the unthinkably erotic sex she'd shared with Garon and Baelor last night, she couldn't help but feel giddy and hot, her pussy oozing desire beneath the hem of her silk dress, even growing tattered as it was.

She'd often wondered about the existence of common villagers in Caralon, wondering what drove them, what kept them happy even though they hadn't many choices in life or the many luxuries she did in the fortress. But now she thought she knew. They could fuck day and night if they wished, they could bed each other copiously with no one to worry or judge or fret over it in any way. And an hour of good sex, she'd learned, was enough to keep her happy all day.

The tavern had been left excessively messy last night, so it took her the entire day to make it ready for another night of drinking. When Garon came in near dusk, looking flushed, a bit windblown and inexorably handsome, his eyes seeming to glitter with the late day sun, she was sorely tempted to ask him why they need bother cleaning the place up so much if the customers were just going to dirty it again tonight. But she refrained, for he didn't appear nearly as at ease as during their oh-so-delicious encounter last night.

She was discovering him to be a moody man. Yet she didn't mind it much—so far, he always seemed to turn tender enough with her in the bedchamber. Tender and hot and generous—*beyond*generous—in giving her pleasure. And, as she could not forget, he *had* saved her from being taken home by her father's men. If she served as his slave for fifty years, she feared it wouldn't be enough to repay *that* debt.

"The tavern is clean," she informed him, holding out her arms to motion around her. "Shall I head off to sleep now?" It was what he'd instructed yesterday before the doors had opened for business. And it would suit her fine if tonight turned out like the previous—cleaning, then sleeping, then fucking. In fact, she thought she could become very accustomed to such a life, so long as the man in the center of it all was Garon.

Yet her lover shook his head, not smiling. "Tonight you serve with the other tavern maids, princess."

She raised her eyebrows. Besides the fact that she was already intimidated by her single memory of Sima and Janya, and that she didn't necessarily wish to be ogled by Garon's customers as the other women had been, she had an additional concern. "What if someone recognizes me?"

Another light shake of his head. "You said yourself that unbraiding your hair makes your identity much less obvious. And…" he handed her a cloth sack he'd carried in, "…you'll shed your silk for the night. In more common clothing, you'll look like nothing more than a village girl earning her keep by passing out ale to thirsty men."

Warily, Laela took the bag, wondering what he'd chosen for her and wishing she'd been able to bring some of her more casual garments along when she'd run away.

He pointed to the bedroom. "Go change. There's a comb for straightening your hair, too. Come back looking pretty." He winked lasciviously. "Pretty girls sell more ale."

Laela shut the bedroom door behind her and quietly dressed in a short, brown leather skirt, not unlike one she already owned, and a white…well, it was not a tunic—she wasn't sure exactly *what* one would call it. As best she could tell, she was meant to tie the top between her breasts. It hugged them so tight, though—far tighter than anything she owned. When she glanced down, she felt utterly exposed, the inner curves of the two mounds on clear display. And she didn't have a viewing glass, but she strongly suspected her nipples were visible through the fabric, as well.

For a moment, she was worried by the thought—but then, slowly, she decided perhaps it was not so horrible. The men in the tavern would see her like this, but did they not see other women, like Sima and Janya, this way, too? And when she thought of *Garon* seeing her like this, she could not deny the dampness that warmed her inner thighs.

So rather than fret about something she couldn't change—remembering that she had agreed to do whatever he asked of her—she opened the door and stepped out into the tavern room. "Am I wearing this correctly?"

His eyes riveted on her, his expression dripping with lust. "Ares, yes," he breathed.

She pursed her lips, at once excited by his reaction, yet still concerned about *other* eyes on her. She was trying very hard to be the sensual woman he wanted her to be, but with Garon—and even with Baelor—there had been a certain comfort, a sense of safety she knew she wouldn't feel with just any man. "You can see through the fabric, yes?"

He nodded, grinned. "*Oh* yes."

Despite herself, her pussy seemed to swell beneath her skirt. "And you wish for all your customers to see me this way."

"I told you, pretty girls—"

"—sell more ale," she cut him off.

He gave another short nod.

Just then, the tavern door swung open, admitting a small evening breeze…and Sima and Janya. Both women were giggling raucously and it gave Laela a brief moment to size them up. It was, after all, the only time she'd seen them other than when they'd been kissing and rubbing their bodies together.

The taller one—she didn't know which woman was which yet, since they were always spoken of as a pair—possessed a mane of thick raven hair that fell straight yet wild, all the way to her ass. Her thin, angular face made her pretty yet intimidating, not a woman Laela would wish to quarrel with. She was lean with pert, medium breasts that seemed to stand at attention beneath the thin, fitted tunic she wore, the neckline dropping low between the curves. A sinfully short skirt of brown fur came only to the tops of her thighs, showing off long, muscular, tan legs.

The other woman's hair was a riot of long red locks. Her whole body was more curvaceous, lush, right up to her lips, which appeared swollen. From kissing. Or sucking Baelor's cock, she thought, the vision suddenly planting itself in her head. Her vest of thin, pale fur might have appeared more chaste had it been hooked together at a point higher than her waist, but she obviously intended for much of her lush breasts to be on display. Her black leather skirt was nearly as short as the taller woman's.

"Sima, Janya," Garon said, addressing first the dark-haired tavern maid and then the redhead, "this is Laela."

"Hello," Laela said politely, immediately aware that both were sizing *her* up, as well.

"The new girl," Sima said, her tone indecipherable—neither one of welcome nor dislike.

Janya smiled, a gesture that turned her face truly pretty and highlighted her green eyes. "How did you like cleaning this place all by yourself, sweetie?"

"It was hard work, but...I didn't mind."

"We didn't either," Janya said, grinning wider, "for it was the first time Garon gave us any time to ourselves in..." she rolled her eyes, "...forever."

Garon only laughed and it was clear Janya was teasing him. "You ladies are paid well enough for your toil and you know it."

"And some of it," Sima said in a deep, seductive

voice as she crossed toward Garon, "is work we don't even mind." With that, she reached out, cupping him between his legs and giving a sensuous squeeze. A strange, wild jealousy shot through Laela and she hoped it didn't show on her face.

She hadn't even noticed Janya moving toward *her*. "What Garon and Baelor didn't tell us," the redhead said, giving Laela a long, very thorough once-over, "was how pretty you are."

"Oh," she said, lost for a response. "Um…thank you."

Janya simply laughed. "You seem…" The redhead lowered her chin, clearly trying to puzzle through something about Laela and making her feel as if she were on a stage. "Innocent," she finally decreed. "Naïve. Especially for a girl wearing something that leaves her luscious curves so delectably displayed."

With that, she reached up, running the tip of one finger from Laela's collarbone down the edge of the thin fabric all the way over the curve of her breast to the knot between. Despite herself, the touch left her pussy tingling and had surely made her nipples jut more prominently through the white top.

A glance at Garon found his expression perhaps more lust-filled than Laela had seen it before. Not sure how to respond, she took a nervous step back and reached for a rag to wipe down the nearest table. Undaunted, however, Janya's eyes followed the sway of Laela's breasts as she ran the cloth in circles over the wood and she knew she was wet beneath her skirt—she just wasn't quite sure *why* exactly.

"Laela is to work with you both tonight," Garon announced. "I've a strong feeling," he went on, casting a playful look in her direction, "that she's never served ale to a bunch of rowdy men before, so I'm counting on you to give her instruction until she becomes accustomed to the job."

"It'll be my pleasure to help you out, sweetie," Janya said with a wink that struck her as downright flirtatious, while Sima—still standing too close to Garon for Laela's liking, her arm looped casually around his waist—only glanced over and gave a short nod.

"Sima," Garon said, looking into her eyes with ease, for she was nearly at tall as him, "you don't seem very welcoming to Laela." As had been the case since the women's arrival, his voice was more teasing than truly scolding.

Sima didn't smile, simply replying with a shrug. "She's pretty, and her breasts are *especially* delicious—but you know I've never cared much for the innocent type."

Yes, Garon knew that, all right—it reminded him of Sima's similar reaction to Ellaena, who had not been nearly as innocent as Laela, yet still far less boisterous than the two tavern maids. It was only after Ellaena had left Myrtell with another man that Sima and Janya had first given him comfort after a long night of pouring ale. Since then, their debauchery had become legendary—the reason Garon's tavern drew so many more men than the others in town—and he'd thought it only fair to share such profits with them in higher pay.

At the creak of the door hinges, Garon turned to see two burly farmers amble inside, not quite clean after a day in the fields. "We come for ale and female entertainment. We hear both can be had here," one of them said, a ragged beard dangling from his chin.

Garon nodded. "You've come to the right place," he informed them. "Take a seat and let Janya bring you two goblets."

The same man's eyes narrowed on Laela, and Garon noticed the farmer's companion's gaze drifting in the same direction, the fellow's thicker, darker beard seeming to twitch with anticipation. "When's the entertainment start?"

Despite himself, Garon's back went rigid at the blatant hunger in the man's beady eyes. He chose not to examine his reaction. "Later," he said shortly.

"Bet that'un's got a hot pussy," the first farmer said, still staring at Laela.

Her face went red and Garon froze a little inside on her behalf. The men who drank here were often the raw sort, but not usually *this* raw *this* early. Instinct made him step protectively toward her, as if to shield her somehow, but he quickly realized it was too late for that—Laela's gaze had dropped to the floor, her shoulders hunching inward.

Janya sent a quick, knowing glance to Laela, then to Garon, before she stepped up close to where the men had taken a seat. "You've made me jealous," the redhead said playfully to the big oaf who'd last spoken.

Both men chuckled. "That so?" the first farmer asked.

She nodded. "No one has a prettier pussy than me." With that, she lifted her short skirt just enough to give them a quick glimpse of her fiery-haired mound, then let it drop.

Both men whistled and guffawed their dirty pleasure, and Garon promised himself to thank Janya later for taking the attention away from Laela. That hadn't been his plan for the evening—far from it—and yet he couldn't deny that it pained him to see Laela's discomfort, even that which he'd intentionally created for her.

"That's all you get for now," Janya said, shaking a teasing finger in the farmers' faces, "but the more ale you drink, the more inspired I shall be to show you more pussy."

Soon after, other men came—most were regulars, a few were unfamiliar—and as usual, the room became full as the hour grew later. All the shutters were thrown open to catch the evening breeze weaving its way up through the village from the ocean.

Sima and Janya behaved in their usual reckless fashion—moving freely through the crowd to deliver ale, not minding if the occasional man stroked a breast or reached under their skirts to pinch their asses—Ares knew he'd found a world of profit in two tavern maids who welcomed such uninvited touches, who so loved to display themselves and play at sex in every manner. They were women who took pure delight in titillating others— and titillating others, he suspected, was the greatest form of their *own* excitement.

Laela, on the other hand, clearly tried to stay as close to the serving area as possible, venturing only to the nearest tables to deliver goblets of drink and making her stays there as short as possible. When one friendly young man, accustomed to Sima and Janya, boldly patted her ass, she flinched, moving quickly away.

Garon, of course, wanted to slug the man and hug Laela protectively to him—but he stayed seated, watching from a distance, trying with all that was in him to ignore the tightening of his chest.

Because this meant his plan was working. And because he had to let it. Even if he had been glad of Janya's little rescue of her earlier. He had to harden his heart here, once and for all. He had to be *glad* he'd made Laela uncomfortable. Glad he'd maybe even left her repulsed and a little bit frightened.

Yet he couldn't help noticing she never complained. She never looked to him for help, never looked to him *at all*, now that he thought about it. And she didn't run to Janya for assistance, either, as he might have expected after the other woman's previous kindness. She did what he asked of her without protest. It sobered him, even as he threw back a swig of ale, trying to be drunk enough not to care.

And it also…made him sick. His stomach wrenched

at the look on her face—she was trying to be strong, stalwart, but her eyes couldn't hide her discomfort.

It forced a simple question in his mind.

What in Ares' name was he doing to her? And why? How could he be so damnably cruel?

Because you have to be. You have to show her this is no place for her, no life for her. Not to mention it's no sane life for you to be living, either, harboring such danger in your bed.

And still, as sensible as the explanation seemed to him, he felt like an ass for it, his stomach seeming to curl in on itself more with each passing moment of her distress.

He only let himself be briefly distracted from Laela when a familiar dance began to take place between Sima and Janya. Each night, as the two beauties drank ale and grew aroused by the attention of the customers, they gradually made a point of seeking each other out, sharing passing touches, brushing against each other, reaching out for a sensual caress on the other's belly, hip, ass.

It never took the roomful of men long to notice— some might draw the attention of friends, others simply observed in silence—but a heavy sense of sensuality always developed, seeming to soak the tavern room. And it was soaking the room *now*.

A glance back to Laela, who carefully filled half a dozen goblets on the counter in the rear of the room, revealed that she was probably the only person who *hadn't* noticed the change in the air. Something inside his chest tightened for her, saturating him with regret. He wished everything were different. He wished life hadn't put him in the position of needing to drive her away, of needing to try to shock and offend her.

It was only when Sima and Janya climbed up onto a goblet-strewn table to meet in the center in a long, hot kiss that the crowd began to cheer—and Laela looked up, her eyes landing on the sight responsible for his customers' delight.

Garon studied her expression, those searching hazel eyes, pondering what she felt. Wonder? Horror? Arousal? Repulsion? He didn't know.

He only knew that he couldn't keep on like this. He only knew that, just like the first night when she'd come here, he wanted to protect her, not hurt her. And also like that first night, he wanted to pleasure her. Deeply. He wanted to impart on her still more new pleasures that she'd never known or even imagined. He wanted to deliver her into every form of ecstasy possible.

He made his way through the crowd to the serving area, where she'd resumed filling goblets from a large jug, approaching behind her. He let his hands close warm about her shoulders. "Put that down," he said softly.

She looked up in surprise to find him so close. "But I have to serve—"

He took the jug from her hand and lowered it to the counter. Ran his hands slowly up the lengths of her arms. "No one cares about that now. Trust me."

Their eyes met again over her shoulder and he leaned

nearer still, letting his arms wrap full around her. "Watch," he said, then placed a gentle kiss on her temple and looked back to where Sima and Janya now kneaded each other's soft round breasts for the customers' pleasure.

Janya moaned at Sima's firm caresses, and the sight made Garon go harder, harder than usual when he watched them, because he was holding Laela as he witnessed their passion, because his cock pressed snug against her ass now. *Pleasure, princess—I want to teach you still more about it, want to be the man who gives you all you can handle.*

As Sima yanked apart the low hook on Janya's vest, spreading it to reveal her plump, rose-tipped breasts to one and all, Janya slid her hands up Sima's outer thighs, taking her furred skirt to her slender hips. The room stayed awash with their heat and Garon found himself lowering another kiss—this one to Laela's cheek. "What do you see?" he whispered. "How does it make you feel?"

Janya moaned as Sima's hands closed over her breasts and she drew the other woman into a sensual tongue kiss to the delight of the awed onlookers. The crowd produced still more prodding cheers when Janya hitched Sima's skirt higher, high enough that her cunt was revealed.

Laela took deep, labored breaths within his embrace—he could feel the slight movements of her shoulders against his chest, the rise and fall of her breasts just above his arms. *Lose yourself in lust, Laela. Lust for the other women. But* because *of me.* For *me.* "I feel…confused," she finally admitted.

He leaned closer still, nestled his shaft deeper against her, breathing low in her ear. "Confused?"

Now Sima bent to lick Janya's nipple, bold and pointed. Latching onto it with her mouth, she began to suckle, making Janya groan her pleasure.

"I'm confused because…it makes my pussy pulse. And I don't know why. I am…a woman. And so are they. So…"

Janya lifted Sima's thin tunic over her head to the raucous cries of the men. She molded Sima's high breasts in her hands, then bent to kiss first one, then the other. And Garon merely stayed silent, wanting Laela to take it all in, to let herself become absorbed in it, to quit thinking so much about her preconceived notions of desire and just let herself feel. He'd seen her give herself up to passion with him and Baelor—he wanted to see her give herself up to it again now, completely. *Don't think, my hot little princess, just feel.*

Soon enough, Sima sat back on the table, her legs parted wide, revealing the pink flesh of her cunt, surrounded by dark curls. The customers yelled their encouragement as Janya stroked her fingers through it, then boldly pushed two of them inside her friend. At this, Laela flinched lightly in his grasp, prodding him to hold her tighter, press his erection still hotter and harder into the valley of her ass.

Janya proceeded to slide her fingers in and out, in

and out, Garon's eyes glued to that spot and hoping desperately that Laela felt as entranced by the sight as he. He'd seen it before, of course, many times—but somehow it felt new. Witnessing it with Laela in his arms made it an experience he wanted to have *with* her.

Moments later, Janya slowly, teasingly lifted her own skirt until her cunt, too, was revealed, to the delight of the rowdy men. The two maids leaned back on their asses but moved closer together, Sima lifting one slender leg over Janya's and Janya situating the opposite leg atop Sima's, almost interlocking their bodies—allowing them to press their damp pussies together, moving, grinding. The men went mad, yelling and cheering with reckless abandon, and a goblet banged on a table by way of applause. Both women cast lusty smiles as they rocked their bodies together, fueled—as always—by the excitement they'd created.

"Do you like the way they move together?" Garon asked Laela, stroking the underside of her breast now, unable to keep from it.

"I…I…" Poor, sweet girl—he could sense her trying to understand her own heated reaction, obviously baffling to her.

He slid one hand up her inner thigh, beneath her skirt. "Don't think about whether it makes sense to you, princess. Just tell me what you feel right now."

"I think…my pussy is getting hotter and hotter."

He grinned, lowering a kiss to her hair. "I know. Your thigh is moist."

"And…the way they rub against each other…I don't know why, but…it's making me so excited. It's making me think…"

"Yes?"

"Making me think I must know what it feels like to be a man. For they're lovely together. Just like…just like…"

"What, princess?"

"During my Orientation, my teacher, Aris, showed me her pussy. And that excited me, too, although I didn't understand *that* any more than I understand *this*."

Oh Ares, the beautifully naughty image she'd just planted in his mind. "Sometimes women can be excited by women, Laela. Sometimes men can be excited by men, too. Heat is contagious. And Sima and Janya are incredibly stimulating to watch, for a man *or* a woman. You need not feel confused by it. Just let yourself enjoy." With that, he pressed his fingers to her cunt, again thrilled to be reminded how bare it was, to feel the smooth skin of her mound beneath his fingertips.

Until they sank into her, that was. He slowly, methodically pushed all four fingers between her parted folds and she moaned. Ah, Ares, she was so wet, drenching his hand. He began to stroke, stroke.

"Do you think," she began breathily, "my pussy is as pretty as theirs?"

Using his other hand to cup the underside of her breast, he spoke low and sure in her ear. "Prettier."

"But soon the hair will grow back."

Ah, his sweet little princess. She misunderstood. "It will *still* be prettier," he assured her.

She looked over her shoulder, eyes wide. "Why?"

Because I like you more. I care for you.

No! What was he thinking? Thank Ares he hadn't said it aloud. He *couldn't* care for her. Right now, she was probably the most dangerous woman in all of Caralon for a man to care about.

Garon drew in a deep breath and formed another reply. "Because you get so wet for me, princess," he said, raking his fingers deeper into her, drawing the center one up over the swollen nub at the top. In the middle of the room, Sima and Janya still writhed together on the table, yet all his thoughts focused on Laela now. He peered hotly down over her shoulder at the ripeness of her breasts beneath the thin top, at the way his hand disappeared under her skirt and how her hips moved ever-so slightly against it. "Because your pussy opens so readily for me, and because you're so unafraid of the pleasure it brings you."

Still fucking his fingers, she looked up at him, her eyes melting with innocence. "Am I? Because sometimes, like just now, watching Sima and Janya…"

"Shhh," he said. "Trust me, princess, for a royal girl who just lost her virginity a mere two nights ago, you are incredibly eager and enthusiastic. And I find that…"

"What?" she asked, a hint of a smile painting her face.

He shut his eyes, not quite able to believe he was

going to say this. "I find it beautiful."

She sighed and he knew he would regret this, but at the moment, he didn't care. He stroked his fingers through her wetness more vigorously and with his other hand cupped and molded her breast through the thin cotton weave that barely hid it, raking this thumb across her hardened nipple, again and again. He rained kisses across her neck and listened to her moan, the sound soft enough that only he heard, yet potent enough to turn his stiffened cock even more rigid behind his leather lacings. From time to time he glanced up at Sima and Janya, but they'd lost their appeal for him—his only interest now was to make Laela come. So he whispered it in her ear. "Come, princess. Come for me."

"Oh!" she said, then, "Ah…" and he knew she was tumbling into ecstasy at his command—that simple. It was the deepest pleasure he'd ever experienced outside of his own orgasm.

A moment later, she stilled in his arms and he held her close, utterly amazed by her. He was sorry he'd made her serve the men, but having taken her to heaven in that same crowded room without anyone knowing filled him with a dark, blunt satisfaction. "I love the way you come for me whenever I tell you to," he teased her in a low whisper.

She turned a slow smile up at him. "What you say, I do."

He chuckled warmly at his fervent little slave, then took the opportunity to give her another command. "Go into the bedchamber," he said, finally releasing her from his embrace.

Her lovely eyes sought his. "Are you coming, too?"

It only made sense that he would go with her. That he would fuck her now. That he would complete what he'd just begun with her. But that sense of dark satisfaction had shored up his will again—just a little. She was damnably tempting, so tempting he couldn't quite believe he was finding the strength to resist her—and yet, somehow, he was. For this moment, anyway.

Making *her* come had been his goal, and his joy, just now. And he would have liked to think that made him a more selfless man than he'd realized, but the truth was, touching her, watching her climax, knowing he was responsible for it—it was simply a whole new sort of selfishness for Garon of Myrtell.

"Later," he replied. "For now, sleep."

"But…what about the men, and the ale?"

He shook his head. Not only was his princess sweet and exciting, she was even conscientious, too. "The other girls and I will take care of it. Rest. And then…"

She raised her eyebrows in anticipation. "Yes?"

As a fresh idea became full-blown in his mind, for good or for evil, he gave her a wicked grin. "You shall get a surprise."

CHAPTER SIX

WHEN HE'D SENT her off to bed, it had truly been in an effort to resist her, to show himself that he could, that he was strong enough. And yet, in the very space of a heartbeat, he'd heard himself promising her a "surprise" and he'd known instantly what that surprise would be, and dark lust had pooled low in his belly at the very idea. It *still* pooled there, heavier now.

The truth was, he didn't know if this was one more attempt to offend her and drive her from his home, or if it was his earnest wish to help her find new ways of pleasure. He could only conclude that maybe it was a little of both—or that maybe the outcome of the experiment would provide the real answer to that question.

Like last night, he eased the bedroom door open and stepped inside to light a candle. The glow illuminated the room, and his princess—who lay in sweet slumber on the bed—still wore the revealing outfit he'd given her earlier. He'd never seen anyone look like such a perfect combination of innocence and sin.

"Come in, girls," he said softly, watching Sima and Janya enter. Their clothing was back in place, yet they still appeared in sensual disarray, their hair tousled, lips swollen, eyes hungry. Outside the room, the tavern lay empty and quiet now, and the sense of privacy—just him and three lovely women—dropped over him like a warm fur on an already hot night.

"She is lovely," Janya said, appearing just as taken with Laela as when they'd met earlier this evening.

"Sima?" he asked, hoping the evening might have somehow softened her toward the younger woman.

Like earlier, the dark-haired maid simply shrugged. "I still don't like the innocent sort any more than I did a few hours ago. The only difference now is…soon we shall see just how innocent she wishes to remain, or if she wants to have fun."

"Gentle now," he admonished her. "She is naïve, but she is adventurous, too, and I suspect that before you leave here, your opinion of her will have changed."

Stepping up beside Laela, Garon bent to kiss her awake. Her lips were moist and firm beneath his mouth, meeting its pressure, and she curled one hand around his neck. The simple thrill of her kiss shot through him like fire. "Wake up, sleepy," he said softly.

She eased open tired hazel eyes, smiling. "Is it time for my surprise?"

"Indeed it is. And here they are."

He motioned to the other women, standing at the

foot of the bed, then watched Laela's eyes. As he'd expected, he saw in her gaze both trepidation and arousal. "Do you remember," he said to ease her into the notion, "when you said how lovely Sima and Janya looked together?"

She nodded, her expression still anxious.

"Well, now, my princess, I want to see how lovely *you* look with them."

Laela barely knew how to react, yet her cunt quivered at Garon's words. She'd fallen asleep so tired and emotionally spent that she'd not even tried to anticipate what he might have in mind for her—if only she had, she might have foreseen this and had a chance to mentally prepare. As it was, she had no choice but to follow her instincts. After all, what he said, she did. And his advice from earlier would help her. *Don't think, just feel.* "Very well," she said bravely, peering at him as she sat up in bed.

"You'll do this for me?" he asked.

"Of course. Whatever you wish."

He flashed a knowing look at Sima, who only arched one brow in return, then he smiled down at Laela before bending for another kiss. "I predict, princess, that you're going to make my cock harder than it has ever been before."

"Ever?" she asked, her heart beating a bit faster at the notion.

He nodded, his gaze hot and direct on her. "Ever."

A heady sense of power flooded Laela's body. Knowing this would excite Garon as much as he'd just promised only added to the undeniable wetness already pooling between her legs. Yet she reached out and grabbed his wrist. "I am willing, but...I may need some guidance. I am new at this, you know."

His smile reassured her. "Not to worry. They will be gentle."

She bit her lip and nodded, a fresh sense of anticipation welling in her chest, making her breasts tingle. She looked over at the other two women, seeing their blatant sensuality, feeling it inside her, and sensing Garon's passion at what was about to happen. She was ready to be the woman he wanted her to be.

Slowly, Garon backed away from the bed as Sima and Janya both joined her there. Janya perched at the foot of it as Sima crawled toward her from the far side, each shift of her body as she moved closer holding the promise of pure sexuality. Until Garon had told her earlier that sometimes women wanted women and men wanted men, she'd never known such a thing, so the notion still remained a bit foreign to her—but she couldn't deny how attractive she found each of the women. Janya's large breasts and lush curves drew her the most—she was soft, touchable, her eyes so bright and welcoming, even in the candlelight. Yet Sima's stark, almost cold beauty made Laela wonder what it would be like to be physically intimate with someone so different from her.

As the women sat to form a sort of triangle with her

on the fur, Janya was the first to reach out, tenderly squeezing Laela's knee. The touch of the gentle, feminine hand echoed straight to her cunt and she knew, unequivocally, in that instant that this would not be a toil—no, pleasing Garon this way would be nothing but pleasure.

When Janya leaned in to kiss her, it was far softer than Garon's kisses, even his most tender ones—her lips were as lush as the rest of her—and the meeting of mouths sent a tendril of warmth curling down through Laela's body.

"Me now," Sima said, and Laela sensed a change— Sima suddenly seemed more willing to be with her, and Laela found herself wanting to be bold, wanting to prove herself worthy, not only of her affections but of Garon's, as well. She bent toward the raven-haired woman and met her mouth in a more sensuous kiss. Sima's tongue pushed into her mouth and the kiss grew long, and Laela's pussy wept not only from the sensations of the kiss itself, but from the intensity of Garon's gaze upon them. She could feel his eyes as tangible as any touch, and they inspired and excited her—first to reach out and caress Sima's slender thigh, then to slide her hand brazenly upward, all the way to Sima's breast. She heard both Sima and Garon let out lusty sighs, fueling her. She liked shocking them. And she also liked shocking herself.

She took her time exploring Sima's breast, discovering it to be as firm beneath her touch as it appeared— caressing, kneading, she enjoyed the soft fullness in her palm. She found Sima's nipple, like a bead, pinching it lightly between thumb and forefinger through her fitted tunic. Touching Sima there made her own breasts long for attention.

Letting out a soft sound of arousal, Sima wasted no time reaching to pull the tunic off over her head, just as she'd done earlier in the evening. Only then, Laela had been nothing but a spectator—now she was part of the sensual action.

An *eager* part, her breasts and pussy aching for more. She wanted to show them all how wanton she could be, and as before, Garon's desire fueled her, transforming her curious longings into something more certain and urgent.

She closed both hands around Sima's high, ripe breasts, squeezing, studying her dark brown nipples, and wondering in awe at her *own* arousal, now soaring, her cunt seeming to swell beneath her. Sima sighed and offered a naughty grin at her caresses, her reaction prodding Laela's next move—she leaned in and licked one hard, budded nipple. The tingle echoed from her moist tongue all the way to her own breasts and pussy, and both women sighed.

"My turn," Janya said, and Laela felt bad for neglecting the friendlier girl. Shifting her gaze from Sima to the redhead, she smiled and reached for the hook on Janya's vest. Clearly not intending to be left out, Sima simultaneously reached up to cup Laela's breast, stroking her thumb over the center. And oh, what a heavenly touch—for Laela had grown so excited she desperately needed some stimulation on her *own* body, something to ease the hot aches which were slowly becoming the biggest part of her.

Following her instincts, she turned a kiss to Sima's berry-colored lips, then another to Janya's soft, pliant mouth. Janya reached to mold her free breast and Laela hissed in her breath at the tender new pleasures. She knew the bed beneath her was growing soaked with the juices from her cunt.

Opening her eyes after kissing Janya, she sought out Garon with her gaze. He sat by the door watching, in the same chair Baelor had occupied a few nights earlier. Her man's eyes shone wild, dark, filled with a lust she relished, and she couldn't resist flashing him a dirty smile.

When she looked back to her companions, she found Janya impatiently pushing aside the scant cotton that covered Laela so that her breasts tumbled out in a hot rush.

"Oh, pretty," Janya purred, and before Laela could even react, the other woman moved closer, closer, until Janya's large, soft mounds were rubbing against her own, her nipples lightly abrading Laela's sensitive flesh. She sighed as joy flowed through her in ribbons of tingling heat, and lifted her chest, jiggling back against Janya.

"I'm jealous," Sima whined and, grasping Laela's arm, spun her away from Janya to press her own breasts, smaller but firmer, against Laela's chest. Sima's nipples were harder, longer, and Laela found herself, without planning it, shimmying lightly against Sima, letting their nipples meet and mingle.

Despite the growing sensual fun they were sharing, Laela was surprised when Janya gently pushed her to her back in the bed, firmly taking one of Laela's bared breasts in her hand, the other in her mouth. "Oh Ares," she moaned at the pleasure that assaulted her, then bit her lip in amusement to realize that the two girls were gently fighting over her. And that she liked it.

Not to be outdone, Sima narrowed her gaze and slid one hand up the front of Laela's thigh, making her pussy shiver. "Spread for me," Sima said with a naughty smile, then situated herself between Laela's legs, pushing the brown skirt to Laela's hips.

Both women sighed at the sight of Laela's bared mound. They studied her for a moment, then exchanged looks. "I see you come from money," Sima said, her tone hard to read.

"That's none of your concern," Garon broke in. "Whatever her past, she's naught but a tavern maid now."

As Sima stroked her fingers over the smooth, sensitive flesh between Laela's thighs, Janya said, "Mmm, *I* want to feel it."

But Sima, looking territorial, only shook her head. "Mine first." Then she sunk her mouth to Laela's cunt with great vigor.

"Oh!" Laela cried, then her eyes fell shut as she drank it all in. Maybe she should have been worried that Sima would ask more about her past, but having her breasts and pussy devoured by the two lovely women was more scintillating than she could have imagined.

When she opened her eyes, realizing she wanted to *watch* them devour her, she caught Garon's eyes across the room. They burned wild. Fierce. Lost in lust. She knew her own resonated the same, so she held his gaze as she let one hand sink into Janya's red curls and the other into Sima's dark hair, holding them there, encouraging their ministrations while he watched, then she simply leaned her head back, smiling, knowing how deeply heated he would grow from watching her take her pleasure.

"Ah, Sima," he murmured hotly, "lick that sweet pussy for me."

At the demand, Sima's tongue seemed to work harder at her, and Laela found herself lifting her cunt to Sima's mouth—yet, in that moment, she realized, she did it without particularly thinking about Sima. And when she arched her breast against Janya's capable, suckling lips—she wasn't truly focusing on Janya anymore, either. She simply closed her eyes and let her body react, let it propel itself forward on a reckless path of delight. And if she thought of anything at all, it was Garon. *His* eyes, *his* pleasure. The hot bulge in his pants which she knew must be near to bursting through the tight lacings that held it. And despite the lovely feminine attentions that buffeted her, it was thoughts of her man that increased tenfold every ounce of excitement flowing through her body, every hot ripple, every driving urge for more.

And when the mouths that caressed her most intimate spots lifted her higher, higher, hurtling her toward ecstasy, then finally making her cry out, one name flew passionately from her lips. "Garon! Oh Garon! Yes, Garon, yes! Yes!" In the throes of orgasm, she would have sworn it was Garon's tongue laving her clit, Garon's mouth sucking at her nipple.

After she came down from the hot, hard release, she opened her eyes and gave him a slow, satiated smile— and the grin he returned was delivered with lusty eyes and a smoldering look that promised more to come. Mmm, good. She *wanted* more. She wanted *him*.

Across the room, he pushed to his feet. "Thank you, ladies," he said. "That was lovely. But now it's *my* turn with her."

Despite the heat they'd just exchanged with their eyes, and even despite how much she craved his cock just now, Laela flinched in surprise. Sima and Janya both looked up, apparently shocked, as well.

"I hope you don't think we're finished here," Sima said smartly, still kneeling between Laela's parted thighs.

But Garon only laughed. "Indeed I do. If you're hungry for a man, go find Baelor. If you're still hungry for a woman, you have each other."

Janya, too, looked miffed, her hand still poised on Laela's breast. "But I want *her*. I didn't even get to touch her bare pussy."

His smile was superior and indulgent. "Afraid you've had all you're going to get for tonight. Time to go home now."

"You're serious," Sima said, rising up, hands planted on her hips, eyes blazing.

"Yes, I am." Then he simply pointed toward the door. "Now go."

Laela lay exposed, her clothes in disarray, rather taken aback by Garon's meanness. Of course, she wanted him, but she thought it cruel to invite Sima and Janya to their bedchamber only to send them away before they found their own ecstasy. She watched, still shocked, as the two girls sullenly adjusted their clothing and rose from the bed like children whose tantrums had not gotten them what they wanted.

"You'll be lucky if we ever come back to this Ares-forsaken tavern again," Sima said, pulling her skirt down over her ass, where it had ridden up.

Garon cast chiding eyes. "Now, now, calm down. You know no one will pay you better for doing what you enjoy."

"Even so," Janya said, "you're cruel. You treat us like...like..." Laela sensed Janya's growing frustration. "Tonight, Garon, you're treating us like *most* men treat women in Caralon! And you're not usually that way."

Garon blinked slowly, looking thoughtful, then said gently, "Only for tonight, girls. I don't mean to treat you badly. I just...want to be alone with Laela now, that's all."

Neither woman looked appeased, though, and Laela wanted to calm them if she could. She lifted on her elbows and said, "Thank you. Thank you both. I'm sorry you must leave, but I...well, I enjoyed our time together very much."

Her words seemed to have the desired effect, at least a little. Janya leaned down to bestow soft kisses to her lips, and when she moved away Sima took her place at the bedside, kneeling there to impart a sensual tongue kiss as she reached to twirl Laela's nipple between two fingers in a way that left her hissing with pleasure as the kiss reached its end.

As the two women made their way toward the door, Garon held out open arms. "A hug?" he asked them, his voice playful.

Janya only rolled her eyes and marched past, and Sima ignored him altogether, not even glancing in his direction. She only looked back when she reached the bedroom door to say, "I'll grant you this—you were right. She's not such an innocent little girl, after all. Too bad for you, though, that we want *her* now more than *you*." And then she disappeared through the doorway, her nose lifted in the air for her departure.

Garon grinned after them, clearly not bothered by the drama, then looked back to Laela—who had realized she was overcome with heat, not just from lust and orgasm, but because a particularly hot day had kept the night air too warm. "That was quite cruel of you," she said pointedly, sitting up to begin shedding her disheveled clothing in an attempt to cool down a bit.

"Perhaps," he said, mischievous expression still in place, "but I did it for you."

"I think not. I think you did it for *you*. I was perfectly content to continue experimenting with Sima and Janya. Speaking of which, do you think they will wonder where I came from now?" She couldn't help worrying that Sima might press her or Garon for more information which, of course, they couldn't give.

Garon shook his head. "I think now that she likes you better, she won't care—she'll just want you for sex. And should she ask again, I'll make up a tale—you ran away from a wealthy but abusive father in the north."

On impulse, Laela stood and walked naked out into the tavern, where she knew a basin of water could be found. "All right, that sounds like a good plan."

Garon followed behind her, seeming to forget the conversation. "Where in Ares name are you going? I just got you alone."

She looked briefly over her shoulder. "I'm hot. I need to cool down." And on a mission to do just that, she flung open a set of closed shutters, allowing the full moon to light the room and a bit of fresh air to waft in, as well. Approaching the basin in the serving area, she found a sea sponge, immersed it in the water, and smoothed it refreshingly over her neck and chest. Rivulets ran down over her breasts and belly, making her sigh with relief. "Ah," she said.

A light growl of arousal drew her look back to Garon, who now eyed her like a hungry man who'd just spotted his next meal.

"You appear impatient," she said, enjoying his lust.

He narrowed his gaze on her darkly. "Do you realize what I've suffered tonight, saving my cock for you?"

Running the wet sponge across the tops of her breasts, she tilted her head, curious and surprised. "Saving?"

"I could have fucked any of you tonight at any time—earlier, when the tavern was full, or just now, in the bedchamber. And believe me, I wanted to. My cock is so hard it hurts, princess." He took a step toward her. "But I didn't. Do you know why?"

She shook her head, feeling unduly beautiful and sensual with his eyes on her, with him moving slowly closer to her. When she'd come out here, she'd actually intended to be angry with him for being so mean to the other girls, but now that was long since forgotten.

"Because I wanted *you*, Laela," he said. "*Only* you. Alone. But I wanted to pleasure you first. With my hand. With my eyes. With Janya and Sima." He came nearer still across the shadowy room. "And right now..." He gave her a long once-over. "Ares—do you have any idea how good you look like this, naked and wet?"

She'd never seen Garon quite so...intent. She'd seen him gruff, and she'd seen him playful. She'd seen him be all business and conversely, she'd seen unexpected emotions in his eyes. But she'd never seen him appear so much like a hungry predator, a man who was going to get what he wanted, no matter what it took.

"Do I?" she whispered. She'd just come, moments ago, but the sense of him being on the prowl for her in this new, feral way had her pussy humming again. "Do I look good to you wet?"

He gave a slow, deliberate nod. "And if I were a more patient man, I'd fill a wooden tub and give you a very thorough bath, running that sponge over every delectable inch of your soft body. But my patience for tonight is over, princess. I'm not saving this hot, hard cock another minute."

With that, he enclosed her in a rough embrace, clamped his hands on her ass, and hoisted her up into his arms. Every nerve ending in Laela's body perked to life at being captured in his masculinity. Soft women's bodies—they'd been undeniably pleasant; but she'd known even while they were kissing and touching her that her much greater desire was for a *man*—a *strong, hard-bodied* man. Garon's grip on her was enough to send bolts of lightning darting through her as he pushed her back against the plank wall next to the open window.

His cock crushed against her cunt and she groaned at the feel of the warm, stretched leather pressing at the naked flesh between her thighs, needing what strained underneath. She reached between them, working frantically at the lacings of his pants, bound so tight over his enormous erection.

"Hurry," he breathed. "I can't wait anymore."

She couldn't either. She'd wanted to tell herself she

could, wanted to chastise him for being so selfish—but she needed his cock just as badly as she knew he needed to get it inside her.

Finally, after much tugging, his magnificent shaft popped free, stretching hard and hot up his muscled stomach. Laela wrapped her fist tight around it, guiding it toward the hungry spot between her legs. "Yes, oh yes," she whispered heatedly as the head found her moisture and he began to push. She lifted one leg over his hip, locking it there.

As he sank home, they both cried out—hers a high squeal, his a low grunt of deep satisfaction. Laela looked into his eyes as he began to pump into her, then she bracketed his stubbled face in her hands and lifted her mouth to his.

The inexorably tender kisses from Janya and Sima had been pleasurable experimentation, but *this*, Garon's mouth hard and urgent on hers, was what she needed. His demanding tongue kisses shot fire down through her breasts into her belly as he gripped her ass, lifting her up as she wrapped both legs around him and began to undulate.

"So wet," he whispered. "So slick for me."

She could *hear* how wet she was as he thrust in and out of her. And the measure of his excitement turned her wild in his arms—more than she'd ever been with him before. She wanted to touch him everywhere—her fingernails clawing at his neck and shoulders, his chest and arms. He rained hungry kisses across her face, neck, shoulders.

And then, suddenly, things slowed. A breeze from the window washed over them—lightly lifting her hair, making them both sigh at the refreshing relief it brought. Her quest into the tavern for coolness had made her much hotter instead.

"Look at us," he said softly. "Together." He glanced down between their bodies, where his joined to hers, so she did, too.

"Oh…" she said, taken by the raw beauty of him entering her, thinking of such a prominent part of him being inside her, of their bodies truly being interlocked that way.

It drove her to push against him, still slower than before—a sensual grind that made her eyelids droop with lusty pleasure as her lover offered a deep moan.

As she moved, letting her body guide her, his grip on her ass tightened and he squeezed, providing such exquisite pleasure through her nether regions that it carried her deeper into that place of nothing but hot joy, nothing but working toward the peak. Her clit connected with his body above his incredibly stiff shaft, rubbing perfectly, perfectly. Another breeze wafted in, seeming to constrict her nipples into even harder buds as they kissed, soft, deep, and finally he whispered, "My beautiful princess, come for me."

And like earlier—she did, the orgasm deep and sweet and long, the pulses of pleasure the warmest sensation that had ever echoed through her. Ares help her—was it possible to die of pleasure?

As the climax faded, she leaned forward so that their foreheads met. He delivered a kiss to her lips. "You take me to such incredible places," she said, awed.

He imparted a sensual smile. "Who'd think you'd be able to travel so far without even leaving Myrtell?"

She couldn't help beaming at him, loving the thought. Her sisters had traveled to new, distant homes with their husbands and found happiness, and somehow Laela had always thought it had to be that way—that to find that sort of magic with a man she'd have to journey far into the distance. Yet here, a mere short walk from the fortress where she'd been born and raised, she'd found every sort of excitement she could want with a man—she'd found a new and wonderful place of her very own.

"Tell me you loved it," he said, his smile edging into a more familiar, decidedly wicked one.

"Coming for you? Of course I loved it."

"No, princess. Tell me you loved being with Sima and Janya."

She met his gaze head-on. "You know I did," she admitted.

He grinned hotly. "Yes, but I want to hear you tell me all about it."

She leaned her head back with a dreamy sigh. "They were so soft. So gentle. Their curves felt delectable under my hands, and their nipples against my tongue made my pussy so wet. But...mostly, the thing that excited me was…your eyes. The way you watched. Letting myself do things that…well, that I couldn't ever have imagined doing before tonight, while you watched, was…amazing. It wasn't them who made me come in the bedchamber, Garon. It was you."

Her words left Garon unable to deny what he'd known all along—that she would like playing with Sima and Janya, if for no other reason than that she seemed to enjoy pleasing him so much. And so his earlier question was answered. He *wished* he'd brought the girls to her to frighten her away. He *wished* he'd done it to push her too far, to find the one thing she wouldn't do for him. But the truth was—he'd done it, instead, to pleasure them both.

And now, what she'd just said to him—the words brought him too *much* pleasure, too much attachment to this dangerous girl he was fucking, this dangerous girl he was also *caring* for.

At the moment, he couldn't fight the "caring for her" part, but he *could* indulge further in the fucking. "I want you to feel me so deep, princess," he growled, hotter, more driven, than he'd ever been in his lifetime.

"I do," she purred in her light, pretty voice.

"No. More," he said, then lowered her to the floor and turned her lovely body away from him toward one of the long tavern tables. "Lean over and brace your arms on the wood."

Looking over her shoulder and giving her bottom lip a short, sensual bite, she did as he'd instructed, planting her palms flat, supporting herself against the table so that her sweet round ass jutted toward him in the shadows—inviting him, he thought.

Molding his hands to her soft, curving hips, he plunged his full length back into her in one thrust and she yelled out.

Ah, the connection. The locking with her body. The smell of her sex, the light sheen of perspiration that shone on her back as the moonlight glanced in. He could come so easily right now. But he wasn't going to. No. Because he hadn't fucked her hard enough yet—he hadn't made her feel him in the hot, binding way he knew would bring them the deepest pleasure.

"Do you feel me, princess?" he said through clenched teeth, his breath hot, heart pounding in his chest. "Deep?"

"Oh Ares, yes! So much! So big!" Every word came on a labored sigh, and the response filled him with masculine pride.

"I'm going to fuck you so hard, Laela. I'm going to make you forget anything else but my cock even exists. I'm going to make you scream."

He didn't wait for her answer, instead doing exactly what he'd just promised—he slammed his rod hard into her, again, and again, knowing that the position heightened everything she felt. *Yes, yes.* So wet. So hot. *Thrust. Thrust. Thrust.* She cried out with each hard stroke, and it almost sounded like pain, but he knew it was the most profound pleasure.

"Tell me it's good!" he demanded, his cock pummeling her, driving into her wetness again, again.

"Yes! Oh yes!" she sobbed.

"Tell me you feel it *everywhere*."

She cried out once more, then managed. "Oh Ares, yes! I feel—" *Another plunge.* "—each thrust—" *Another.* "—in my fingers—" *Another.* "—and my toes."

Feel it, princess, keep feeling it. It was his only wish in life in that moment—that she feel him, that she take from him, that she yell out in joy *because* of him. He wanted all of her, in every way, wanted to own her—more than just this slave and master agreement—he wanted her heart, too.

And it was that realization that sent him over the edge, exploding inside her, releasing every ounce of heat and energy that had built in him these past hours—and he knew that *he* was taking from *her*, too, just as much as she was taking from him. What moved between them was pure pleasure…and something more. Something he couldn't, wouldn't, give a name—and now that he'd climaxed inside her, now that the hot tension was easing, he wasn't going to indulge his worrisome thoughts of *caring for her* any longer.

She turned in his arms, flashing her innocent smile—and Ares, he found that more alluring than anything else she could possibly do, and she wasn't even trying.

"You've worn me out tonight," she said.

He ran his hands down the length of her soft, beautifully bare arms then took her by the hand. "Come to bed, princess."

Although it was only as they lay down together atop the fur that he realized, despite his weariness, he was too wide awake to sleep. Odd—usually, like most men, he could drift off quickly after sex. He'd opened the shutters in the bedroom now, too, for the breeze, but admitting the moonlight as well, and so he found himself watching her as she closed her eyes, settling in for the night.

He studied her pale cheeks, pinkened slightly from fucking. He studied her long, dark lashes and her soft, pouting lips. The tips of her breasts still puckered, even now, tempting his mouth, but he knew she needed to rest.

Yet then his eyes fell on something he'd noticed about her the first time he'd met her, and he realized he'd never seen her without it. She lay naked but for the odd cat's face pendant at her neck. "Why do you never take this off, princess?" he murmured in the shadowy room, reaching out careful fingers to touch the ribbon it hung from.

She smiled sleepily, and he was selfishly pleased to find she was still awake. "It was a gift from my mother for my last birthday."

"Ah," he said, hearing the light air of melancholy in her voice. "You must miss her." He knew that girls and their mothers often seemed closer than any other familial relationship he knew of.

"Very much," she admitted, reaching to touch the cat's face. Their fingers mingled there, at her throat. "She loves me."

I love you, too.

He went stiff at the insane thought, then pushed it back in his mind, as far back as possible, as he drew his hand away. "Unusual gift," he said instead.

She simply shook her head against the pillow, eyes still shut, a small smile unfurling on her pretty face. "It's supposed to be my cat, Midnight. He's still at the fortress. I hope someone's taking care of him, feeding him. I miss him terribly, too."

He couldn't help being confused. "Your *cat*? And this cat—it needs to be *taken care of*?" He'd never heard of such a notion.

Finally, she opened her eyes, the hazel color looking nearly as green as the cat's gem eyes in the dim light. "I know most people only see cats as wild animals that keep mice away and kill birds, but…Midnight was the runt of his litter and his mother didn't want him. And I've always had an affinity for cats, odd as that may sound. I brought Midnight to the fortress and he was my constant companion…before I ran away."

He couldn't help chuckling at the peculiar idea. "Leave it to you, princess, to charm a cat into a companion."

She delivered a playfully accusing look in the darkness. "What does *that* mean?"

He shook his head, laughing. "Only that I think you could charm…well, anybody. To do anything you wanted."

Her expression softened. "Is that so?"

He gave a short nod, and realized, with regret, that the late hour and his warm feelings had gotten the best of him yet again. Time to put a stop to it, so he narrowed his brow and spoke gruffly. "But that doesn't mean you're not still my slave."

"May I tell you a secret?" she asked.

Say no. Quit indulging her, once and for all. "Yes." This was a mistake.

"Strange as it sounds, I rather *like* being your slave, and I fear I would miss it if I suddenly could not be."

He wanted to kiss her. Desperately.

But this was going way too deep, getting far too close to the very danger he was trying to avoid. "Goodnight, princess," he said simply, turning the other way in bed, trying not to feel her, smell her, sense her lovely presence.

Still, her pretty voice came in his ear just the same. "Goodnight…master."

CHAPTER SEVEN

G ARON TOTED A heavy keg of ale through the open tavern door, lowering it to the counter in the serving area. It was the last of three he'd carried from the delivery wagon up the way. Once he caught his breath, he yelled out, "Princess, where are you?"

Despite himself, after last night, he was anxious to see her. Try as he might to will her away, last night had been eye-opening. He still wasn't ready to accept some of the crazy thoughts that had wafted through his mind during their more intimate moments, but he couldn't refute that he admired her sensual abandon and the way she met every challenge. And that each and every time she surprised him, she also...*moved* him, making him feel something new and sobering deep down inside.

Ares, quit thinking this way. Hadn't he just told himself he wouldn't indulge those thoughts?

"Still in bed, sleepy girl?" he called, leaning through the doorway.

But the bed lay empty, the fur covering stretched tidy

across it. A glance to a hook on the wall revealed that her green silk dress no longer hung there, and he couldn't deny to himself that if she had left the tavern, he was glad she hadn't worn the skimpy top he'd made her wear last night. She'd looked delectable in it, but letting other men see her that way—*that* had been a mistake. One of many he was making lately, it seemed.

That's when it hit him. If she had left the tavern…

She'd *never* left the tavern since coming here a few days ago.

He'd assumed she'd be too afraid to show her face in daylight, fearful that someone from the fort might be in the village, that she'd be recognized.

So where would she go that was important enough to draw her from the relative safety of the building?

Or…dear Ares, what if someone had *taken* her? A blade of panic sliced through his heart.

Turning, he stalked toward the door and out into the pathway that wove through the village. The first person he met was Baelor, heading toward him with a bright smile.

He grabbed the younger man's shoulder in such a way that it wiped the grin right off his face. "Have you seen Laela?" His voice came too harsh, but he didn't care.

Baelor flashed a questioning look. "Yes. Why? What's wrong?"

"Where is she?"

"At the ocean."

Garon let his brow narrow. "At the ocean? What in

Ares name is she doing *there*?"

Baelor raised his eyebrows, as if to say *calm down.* "Just going for a walk, Garon. Said she liked the sea. What's the matter with you?"

It was as if a blanket of relief dropped over him. He finally released Baelor's shoulder from his grip. "Sorry. I just…feared the worst. Feared Enrick's men had come back."

"Oh," Baelor said somberly. "No, nothing like that." Then he lowered his chin and gave Garon a sizing-up look. "And if they did, you would be upset because…?"

Garon considered telling his friend the truth, but since he couldn't even quite admit it to himself and was still hoping his feelings would fade to normal, he answered stiffly. "She's my slave and I'm not even close to being done with her. Besides, if they find her in my tavern, chances are I'll take the blame."

Baelor tilted his head, looking thoughtful. "On the night we shared her, you seemed…"

"What?" Garon snapped. "I seemed what?"

Baelor took a step back, but spoke frankly. "Fond of her."

Garon forced a shrug. "Perhaps. But she's also my property, and someone who is putting me in danger, both of which are far greater issues than whether or not I like the girl."

With that, he started past his friend.

"Where are you going?"

"To the beach," he tossed over his shoulder.

"Funny," Baelor murmured behind him, "You'd think if the girl's such a danger, you wouldn't be so anxious to track her down and bring her home."

Garon pretended he didn't hear and kept walking, mainly because he had no sensible reply. If he was honest with himself, his mind had been messed up about her since the moment they'd met. He wanted to enslave and punish her—or did he just *want* her? He wanted her to leave—but he pleasured her so much that he knew she'd stay. Nothing he thought or did regarding her seemed to make much sense except in the very moment he was thinking it or doing it. And still his steps led him onward, through the outskirts of Myrtell, over the dunes that had only partially reclaimed the remains of the Before Times structures that had once lined the shore, and down onto the empty beach.

Empty…except for the pile of green silk that made a small mound on the pale sand. He narrowed his gaze on it, trying to make sense of what he saw.

Was she…in the water?

Apparently so. Without her dress. His cock rose slightly.

So his princess was full of still more surprises. She swam in the ocean—naked. Unheard of. But he was still very glad he'd come.

Bypassing the pile of silk, he walked down through the soft sand toward the gently rushing tide and looked out on the water to find a head bobbing in the waves. He thought to call to her, but instead, simply watched her for a moment.

As the whitecapped swells rolled inward, she leapt up and over them, seeming to make a game of it. Silly little princess. Even so, he enjoyed watching the way her long, wet mane of hair clung to her back, the soft pale expanse of her shoulders visible on either side. When she dove over a small wave like a lovely, curvaceous fish, disappearing smoothly beneath the water, the white flash of round ass hardened him still more.

"What in Ares' name do you think you're doing out there?" he yelled when her head emerged to break the surface again.

She looked around with a start, then smiled when she saw him. "I'm swimming!" she called merrily back.

He tried not to grin at her easy, infectious exuberance. "Yes, I can see that. But…why?" The beach was for launching boats and bringing in fish and lobsters and sea sponges. Given the sun and tide, it was a harsh place.

"I *love* to swim. Especially when the weather is so hot—it's a wonderful way to cool off."

"Your father let you swim in the ocean?" He found that hard to believe. It was hardly a civilized activity, and certainly not for the royal.

"Of course not," she replied on a laugh. "But my sister Teesia and I used to sneak to the ocean anyway."

He drew closer to the water's edge and she moved inward, too, on the sloping sand, rising from the water just enough that the round tops of her breasts shone porcelain beneath the sun—until a wave swept around her shoulders, knocking her off balance just slightly, making her laugh.

Clearly, the girl did not have a healthy fear of the sea as most people did. "And just what is so pleasurable about swimming?"

"Well, as I said, it cools the body down on a day like today." Indeed, the sun burned down hot overhead, the cruelest part of summer definitely upon them now. "When we were young girls, I suppose it was an adventurous, forbidden thing to do. I was mainly following my older sister's lead. But I found there is…a certain freedom, a certain comfort, in floating about in the water, feeling it caress your skin."

He made no effort to hide a wicked grin. "If you want your skin caressed, princess, I can think of a better way. And should you get a sunburn on those pretty shoulders and delectable breasts, well…my caresses will not be so pleasurable then, will they?"

She cast a playful smirk. "Don't worry—I don't plan to spend the whole day here. It's simply a quick dip to freshen me."

"You could drown," he warned.

Even over the distance that separated them, he saw the roll of her eyes. "I swim quite well."

He granted her a soft smile. "So I see."

"And there is also a certain thrill in knowing the ocean is so much bigger than oneself, so much more powerful."

He laughed. "And if you want something powerful,

princess…" He pointed toward the bulge in his pants.

The gesture drew a large smile from the girl in the water. She'd moved close enough to shore that her breasts were visible, her hard, wet nipples seeming to bob atop the gentle waves. "Bring it here," she said.

"What?" Had he heard her correctly?

"Bring your cock here. Come into the water with me," she prodded.

"Why?" He, too, had snuck off for an occasional ocean swim as a boy, but those days were long behind him.

"I want you to fuck me," she said, her voice going as silky as the dress she'd abandoned on the sand, yet even over the sound of the rushing tide, he heard the words with clarity. "Here. In the ocean. I want to be…a water nymph for you."

With that, she smoothed her palms up her torso and over her breasts, which glistened with moisture beneath the sun. His rod appreciated the gesture, stiffening yet further, so as to press uncomfortably against the leather lacings above his crotch. As he'd noticed last night in the empty tavern, she looked irresistibly lovely when wet, her curves seeming to shimmer in a way that begged for his touch.

"A water nymph, eh?" he said, drawn still closer now without thought, so that the sudsy tide rolled up over the toes of his boots. "You want to be a mermaid for me, princess?"

They shared a knowing smile, a smile that spoke of a

knowledge few others had, because they both happened to be more learned in the Before Times texts than the average Caralonian. "You're grandfather *was* well read."

"As are you, princess."

She gave her pretty head a slight tilt, her lower lip a thoughtful little bite. "Only, I don't see that a mermaid could have a pussy, could she?"

The notion drew a boisterous laugh from him. "That makes me glad you're not really a mermaid."

"Me, too," she said, her expression growing sensual, seductive. She took another step higher on the sand, and when the tide receded, her lovely cunt was put on display for him as she said, "Because I *do* have a pussy, and it's very hungry for you."

She stroked her longest finger teasingly through the bare slit, offering a lusty smile that left him helpless. He had no choice but to start yanking off his boots, shrugging free from his vest, letting each item drop on the beach behind him. The potent heat of her eyes burned through him hotter than the sun as he worked the ties on his pants, finally pushing them down to reveal his hard length.

As he took one tentative step into the cool water, bared from head to toe, he gazed on her lovely nudity with a grin. "It's a good thing for you that the rest of Myrtell does not enjoy swimming."

She returned the flirtatious smile. "And why is that?"

"Someone could come upon us like this at any time."

She gave her head a saucy tilt. "And you think I

would care?"

"You wouldn't?" He lowered his chin in speculation.

"I am not the same girl who came running into your tavern a few days ago, Garon," she said, and indeed, the look in her hazel eyes was that of a bold, confident woman—no longer the little girl he'd saved from her father a mere three evenings prior. He'd thought he wanted her then—hell, he had *definitely* wanted her then—but this, now, was something much more powerful than that.

As he moved toward her through the foaming sea water, he forgot his wariness of the ocean and how odd it seemed to be wading into the vast body of water to reach her—all that mattered was, in fact, *reaching her*.

She took playful steps backward, easing slightly deeper again into the sea, her provocative gaze summoning him just as much as her wet body.

"Stay where you are," he said on a bit of laughter.

She flashed a defiant grin, shook her head, and took another step back as a soft wave rose around her waist, lapping at the underside of her breasts.

"How can I fuck you, princess, if you keep moving away from me?" He'd forgotten how heavy ocean water was, how difficult it was to walk into it with any speed, and she seemed miles away from him.

"All right, fine," she said with a cute giggle, "I shall wait here." She stood in water up to her waist and, dear Ares, he didn't think he'd ever seen a lovelier sight than the woman who had teased and cajoled him into the shushing tide.

As a wave rose, wetting his cock, he shivered slightly, but his steps became easier now that he'd descended deeper, and the shifting sand beneath his feet led him closer to her. Finally, he slid damp palms over her hips, up her sides, until he cupped the outer curves of her breasts, stroking his thumbs across their taut, pink centers. The hard beads felt delectably lovely against his thumbs and he stroked them, then twirled them, pinching lightly, making a hot sigh erupt from her throat.

Drawing him down into a kiss, she moaned into his mouth just as their tongues met. He pressed his impatient cock against the juncture of her thighs, molding his palms over her large breasts, and let the pleasure of so many connections with her body assail him.

As they touched and kissed, the water moved between them almost like a third person, and Garon suddenly understood what she meant about the waves caressing the skin. The sea lapped gently at their hips and asses, coming up onto their bellies where his hardened flesh met with her softness.

When her small, wet hand wrapped around his thick length, he groaned and gave her a wicked smile. "Do you know what you do to me?" he murmured.

She nodded with playful confidence. "I tempt you into the ocean. See how fun it is?"

"Yes, princess, I do," he replied, curling his hands around her ass at the water's surface. He stroked one long finger into her pussy from behind. Whether she was wet from the sea or wet from her juices, it didn't really matter—she was drenched, soft around his finger when he gently slipped it up inside.

"Mmm," she purred, rubbing her slit against his cock as her pointed nipples brushed over his chest. She pressed kisses to his neck, his jaw, driving him to lean his head back at the scintillating pleasure. "Fuck me, Garon," she breathed up into his ear, her voice throaty, needy. "Please fuck me."

"Your wish is my command," he said, quoting a common line from the Before Times tales his grandfather had told him as a boy.

She smiled, appearing familiar with it, as well.

Who was the slave now? he wondered briefly. But he didn't really care. Little seemed to matter at the moment except getting inside her.

With his hands still circling her bottom, he lifted her in his arms—noting how the water made her more buoyant—and lowered her slowly, surely onto his erection. They both moaned as her cunt sheathed him with wet ease, taking him to the hilt. They stayed still a moment—she pressed her forehead to his, as if trying to adjust to the pleasure of their physical bond. "I am so very glad," she whispered, the words barely audible over the sweeping tide.

He sensually massaged her ass beneath the waves. "Glad of what?" Their heads still touched.

"Glad of everything. Glad I am royalty. Glad my

father tried to marry me to an old man. Glad I ran away." She looked up, into his eyes. "For it all led to this moment. And what I feel right now, Garon…" She shook her head lightly. "I wouldn't trade it. I wouldn't change a thing, even if I could. This moment, with you, is as close to heaven as I'll ever come before death."

Her words moved through him like a hot shock of lightning—almost paralyzing, but in a way that was inexorably…*good.* "Me, too," he murmured, pressing his mouth over hers, drinking of her as, below, their bodies slowly began to move, to grind.

"Mmm, yes," she sighed, thrusting her sweet pussy against him, writhing beautifully in his grasp. He thrust back, wanting her to feel his cock deep, as deep as he could go, but he kept his own movements gentle, knowing she'd find her ecstasy quicker if he simply let her ride him.

"That's right, princess," he whispered hotly, every nerve ending in his body tingling with sexual energy. "Work your pretty little pussy on my cock. Ride me until you come. Ride me until your cunt explodes in pleasure."

Her breath was hot, her eyes heavy-lidded, her breasts swaying as she moved on him, seeking that sweet release. "Oh, Garon," she breathed. "Yes, Garon, oh yes."

Her gentle murmurings sent still more intense pressure to his shaft and her climbing heat seemed to melt off of her and onto him. "Come for me, my princess," he urged, then stroked his middle finger down over the fissure of her anus beneath the water.

"Oh…" she moaned, eyes shut, clearly lost in pleasure.

He stroked again, and again, then pushed the tip of his finger inside, until it caught there.

"Oh!" she cried, her eyes bolting open to meet his.

"Come," he said. No smile this time. Nothing soft. Everything hot and hard. "Come. Now." Then he plunged his finger deeper in her ass.

She gasped, her eyes wide and wild—and then her head dropped back, her breasts arched forward and her pussy undulated slow but firm against him. She sobbed softly, her cries meshing with those of seabirds in the distance, and by the time the cries faded, Garon could no longer control himself.

He thrust deep, hard, rough, jolting her.

She clung to his neck.

He plunged his finger still deeper in her tight ass, aware that she was meeting hard strokes both from the front and the back, from his cock, from his finger. Her nails clawed lightly into his shoulders as he fucked her faster, the rhythm rising, rising—until she yelled out and came again in his arms when he least expected it, bucking violently, scratching at his back.

"Ares," he bit off through clenched teeth as he shot his pleasure deep into her warm cunt, each pulse like a trip to heaven and back—again, again.

The orgasm left him so weak that he nearly released

her into the water surrounding them, but he managed to hold tight, resting his forehead on her shoulder. The sun blazed down on them and the soft waves lapped gently at their torsos, but Garon didn't feel it—he felt nothing but Laela. She was his slave, she was his princess, and she was becoming everything in between.

FOR LAELA, LIFE had come to be all about the joy of sexual exploration. In the weeks that followed, she barely even found time to worry about what might be happening at the fortress, missing home, or anything else. In some ways, she thought, it was as if she hadn't even existed before coming here, to Garon's bed.

She still toiled to clean the tavern during the day, readying it for the night's business ahead, but now Garon helped with the work, making it feel more as if keeping the business running was an endeavor they embarked upon *together*.

Sometimes Baelor helped, too—showing up at midday to help Garon transport kegs or jugs of ale. One day, the two men carried all the tavern's tables outside, allowing Laela to mop the wooden floor. Yet when she joined them behind the building to help wash down the tables with water and soapy sponges, her dress grew wet and clingy, and before it was over, Garon had dragged her inside to the bedchamber, leaving Baelor to the task all by himself, something he'd teasingly complained about for days after.

Garon bought Laela a pale, furred vest to replace the too-sheer blouse, and she wore it with her brown leather skirt, sometimes serving ale at night with Sima and Janya—but she stayed close by her lover's side, and it became known to the patrons that she belonged to *him*, so the men reserved their flirtatious touches for the other women.

Often, Laela would carry a goblet to Garon and curl up on his lap to simply enjoy the general camaraderie of the tavern at night. She relished the protective hand he would curl over her ass or high onto her leg, glad not only for others to see their affection but also pleased and thrilled to feel so possessed by him. She only hoped that the possession had transformed into something deeper now. Although he never said so, she found herself daring to wish that she had become *more* than a possession, more than a mere object of work and sex.

"Shall I fetch you another goblet?" she asked him one night as she perched on his thighs, one arm lying comfortably around his shoulders.

"That would be good, princess, yes," he replied, his eyes glittering on her in the candlelit room. Around them, men talked and laughed, others flirted with Sima and Janya, but all she really saw was Garon's seductive smile, the dark stubble on his jaw, the wayward lock of blond hair that drooped mischievously over his forehead.

As she moved to the counter, Sima swayed toward her in another sinfully skimpy skirt of dark brown fur, frayed at the hem to make it so short at some points that

Laela thought she might catch a glimpse of Sima's cunt as she moved. Although Garon had never again suggested she be intimate with the two women, Laela had grown accustomed to watching Sima and Janya entertain the men with each other. Thus, she'd also grown accustomed to the sight of both women's pussies, so even though she didn't see Sima's right now, she couldn't help but envision it as her skirt threatened to reveal her mound with each sensual step she took.

"Eh, Sima," one of the men—a newcomer who'd only been in the tavern the last few nights—called from a nearby table, "how come you never touch *that* one?" He pointed to Laela, where she stood pouring Garon's ale from a clay jug.

Sima laughed. "Because that one is *his*," she replied, pointing to Garon, who wore a wicked grin of arousal. "And since Janya is busy just now,"—she, in fact, was straddling a burly man in a chair in the back of the room—"you shall have to be patient. But as soon as Janya is done, I'm sure she will want a sweet taste of this." She lifted the ragged hem of her skirt the few inches it took to put her cunt on display. The men cheered hungrily as Sima raked one long, slender finger through her slit, leaned forward to let the nearest man take that finger into his mouth, then withdrew it and turned back to her work.

"Aw, now, Garon's a reasonable fellow. He won't mind a bit of sharing. Will you now, Garon?" Clearly, the man who spoke—older than Garon, but a clean sort who Laela suspected worked at some trade in the village—had known Garon a long, comfortable while.

Laela's gaze flicked from Sima, who licked her lips as she looked Laela over as if she were a tasty bit of meat, to Garon, whose teasing smile brimmed with amusement. "Whatever she likes," he said, and she knew he meant it. She could also tell, from the very expression on his face, that he would welcome such an indulgence—and the knowledge left her pussy moist.

On the night she'd become intimate with Sima and Janya, she'd experienced true pleasure at their ministrations—and she couldn't help being aroused by the notion of experimenting further, especially given the heat in Garon's gaze. True to Garon's prediction, Sima had never again questioned Laela's past and seemed only interested in the sexual possibilities.

She peered over at Garon, licked her upper lip, and let him know without words—*this is for you, lover.*

It was for him, and it was also for her. *Her* delight with Sima would delight *him* in turn. And his pleasure from watching would ricochet back onto her even *more* powerfully.

She looked at Sima with her tall, thin stature, her dark beauty, her nipples jutting through a thin white blouse that stopped above her navel, those legs that stretched on forever—and she wanted her.

For Garon. For herself.

And even for all the men in this room.

She wanted her because Garon was not demanding

she do it. She wanted her because she knew she could take pleasure from Sima, and because she wanted to show her man that she understood pleasure *fully* now, that he'd opened her to a deep joy she'd have never known otherwise.

The two women came together slowly, sensually, their bodies barely grazing one another until Laela leaned in, open-mouthed, for a kiss.

The men cheered their arousal, and though Laela could not see Garon in that moment, she felt his gaze and let it run all through her like warm, slow syrup.

Feeling suddenly bold, fearless, she followed the urge to reach up and touch Sima's breast. The other girl sighed and smiled sensually down at her as Laela gently squeezed the high, firm globe, raking her thumb across the hard peak. Heat radiated from her hand down through her arm and body, and any last vestiges of shyness that might have remained inside her fell away, prodding her to undo the two hooks between Sima's breasts and push the thin fabric aside to grasp both taut mounds.

The men's raucous comments and cheers persisted, but Laela's world became Sima—and Garon. Was *he* cheering? Sighing? Moaning? She had no idea, but in her mind, yes, he was. In her mind, he whispered in her ear, telling her how beautiful she was with Sima, telling her he wanted more—more touching, more kissing—telling her he wanted her to follow her every whim without thought or reservation.

Sima moaned as Laela tenderly kneaded and caressed her lovely breasts—tan from exposure to the sun. *I should let mine tan, as well,* she thought. Garon was such a natural man, natural and hard-working and earthy like everyone else in Myrtell, and she knew instinctively that he would enjoy seeing her skin grow sun-kissed like Sima's.

On impulse, she bent to lick one nipple, delightfully hard on her tongue, then let her lips close around it, gently sucking.

Sima's sighs from above her prodded her on as her hands ran through Laela's hair.

Finally releasing the hard bud from her mouth, she smiled up at the other girl, then sank her tongue to the opposite nipple, letting it circle and twirl about the dark, rosy bead. "Oooh," Sima moaned, her eyes filled with naughty joy as she looked down on Laela. But it was not Sima's gaze that fueled her. *Watch me, Garon,* she thought, laving Sima's pretty nipple, concentrating on making it wetter and wetter. *Watch me.*

When finally she rose from Sima's breasts, Sima wasted no time undoing Laela's vest hooks. As Sima pushed the fur aside, seizing the ample mounds, Laela was reminded exactly where she was, suddenly feeling the hungry, lusty eyes of all the men in the room. Unlike the night when Garon had made her wear her skimpy top to serve them, though, tonight their rapt stares made her hot inside, so hot that she knew her own juices were leaking from her beneath her skirt. She instantly understood how all those eyes fueled Sima's and Janya's passion—and yet, even so, the man whose eyes she felt the most remained Garon.

As Sima molded Laela's breasts, too large to be contained in the dark-haired girl's hands, Laela looked over at him and knew her daring had succeeded in exciting him beyond all measure. His mouth had dropped open slightly and he appeared near to salivating. Despite herself, she drank in the power it gave her and realized she wanted more. She loved being his slave—but in this moment, just for now, she wanted to make him *her* slave.

"Kiss them," she said to Sima.

All the men reacted, sighing in awe, but she kept her gaze on Garon, whose eyes now locked on her bared chest.

Sima didn't hesitate to lean in, bestowing soft, lovely, titillating kisses on first one erect nipple, then the other. Laela watched her, watched the feminine hands mold her, watched the feminine lips gently kiss and lick her. Pleasure radiated throughout her body and she let it own her, let herself drink it in, soak it up, as she watched the other woman continue laving the hard peaks of her sensitive breasts, until her cunt hummed with deep, heated pleasure beneath her skirt. She wondered if her juices were yet running down her inner thighs.

More. Surprise him more. Surprise yourself more. Don't think. Just indulge. Let the pleasure surround you, swallow you. Become a part of it. Become pure pleasure.

She continued caressing Sima's breasts as Sima pleasured hers, too—until she finally pushed Sima away from her. She didn't let the taller girl's look of shock—maybe even anger—disturb or dissuade her. She'd make her happy again soon enough.

Laela shoved Sima gently until her back met the wall. Then she kissed Sima's breasts...and Sima's stomach. She slowly dropped to her knees and let her hands slide up the fronts of Sima's strong, slender thighs...until the other girl's tiny skirt was pooled at her hips, her cunt on lovely display.

Obviously sensing what was to come, Sima gazed down into Laela's eyes, then lifted one foot to the stone ledge below the hearth Garon used to heat the place in winter. The move parted the dark, thin curls that protected her pussy so that her flesh shone pink and wet in between.

Laela used the fingertips of both hands to gently touch Sima's outer lips, to spread her farther, to explore. She could smell Sima's moisture as it dampened her fingers, sexuality oozing from her.

She ran the tip of her thumb over Sima's clit, eliciting a light moan from above. Around her, the room had grown strangely quiet.

"Lick it," Sima said softly.

Laela leaned in to rake her tongue sensually through the pink folds of Sima's pussy, sensing the woman above her shuddering at the sensation as she drank in the deep scent of her and absorbed the salty taste.

She licked again, letting herself feel the soft flesh

beneath her tongue, ending at the swollen little nub at the top. Soft. Slick. Salty-sweet.

That's when two strong arms encircled her from behind and she raised her gaze, startled, as Garon picked her up and tossed her over his shoulder as if she were a sack of cornmeal.

"Sorry, Sima," he said, his voice deep, husky, "but someone else will have to finish the job. I'm sure you won't have trouble finding volunteers." Then he stalked toward the back of the tavern and through the door into the dark bedchamber, toting Laela the whole way.

Laela heard the door slam behind them just before he dropped her onto the fur-covered bed. Her heart beat like a drum in her chest. What was happening? Had she misread his response?

A second later he was on her, his body weighing hers down, his cock pressed hard between her thighs. She could see him only in shadow, by the pale moonlight admitted through open shutters. "What in Ares name *was* that?" he bit out.

She let her arms close cautiously around his shoulders as his hands gripped her breasts, tight. "Are you angry at me?" she asked, stomach churning now.

He drew back slightly—and she saw the astonishment in his eyes. "Have you lost your sanity, princess? You just gave me the most enormous erection of my life."

Relief flooded her and she smiled in the dark. "Good. You taught me that watching could bring deep pleasure, so I wanted to thrill you by touching her, kissing her."

He lowered a hot, hard kiss to her mouth. "When you licked her pussy I nearly came in my pants."

"I…wanted to see what you feel like when *you* lick *me*. I wanted to know what you taste."

The sound that left him was a hungry growl and his next harsh kiss left her lips nearly bruised. Her cunt wept for attention now and he seemed to know it, for he worked his way briskly down her body with more rough touches and wild kisses until he was shoving her skirt up, bringing his mouth down on her aching pussy.

"Oh Ares!" she cried at the brutal pleasure.

His tongue followed, licking furiously, again, again, until his mouth latched onto her clit, sucking hard and relentless as she thrust responsively at his face. Without thought, she molded her own soft breasts in her hands, letting the nipples become pinched between her first two fingers, as he curled his hardened palms beneath her ass.

She lifted to him, lifted, lifted, hard and near the point of climax, when he thrust a finger into her anus and sent the orgasm barreling through her like great waves rolling on the ocean, crashing through her cunt and outward. "Oh Garon," she sighed. "Yes, Garon, yes."

She'd not even faded to normal when he plunged his hard cock deep into her. *Oh Ares!* Both cried out and he murmured, "So wet, princess, so hot and wet inside."

Beyond the door, they could hear the vague sounds of men cheering, could hear the usual boisterous comments, evidence that Sima had either drawn Janya away from her man in the back of the room or that she'd found a man of her own to deem worthy. Garon drove into Laela hard, hard, hard, each thrust jolting her and filling her with the deep, abiding pleasure of being his. She'd enjoyed the hint of power she'd stolen away from him for a few minutes, but was just as happy to have it reclaimed by him, too.

Fill me. Fuck me. Make me yours. She already *was* his, in her heart, in his mind—she knew that. But maybe she wanted the same in *his* heart, too.

Yet she tried not to think—only to feel. That wondrous shaft pummeling her so marvelously. The strength and masculinity of the man behind it. *Yes, yes!*

Long, hot moments of profound joy later, he spilled himself in her with a mighty groan, then collapsed atop her body, their disheveled clothing pooling and stretching between them. In the tavern, the sensual party continued, but in the bedchamber, the only sound was Laela whispering in Garon's ear. "May I ask you something?"

He didn't bother looking up, but she felt his breath warm on her neck. "What is it?"

"If you liked watching me lick her pussy so much, why did you stop me?"

He turned to face her in the dark and she more felt than saw his smile. "Because I had to have you, my naughty little princess, and though I don't mind a bit of sharing, when I fuck you, it has to be you and me, alone."

She tilted her head on the fur beneath, confused. "What about when you invited Baelor to join us? He fucked me, too."

After a barely discernible bit of hesitation, Garon's voice grew slightly more grim. "That was then. This is now."

Could it be? she wondered. *Could* he feel something for her in his *heart?* Something that made their sex feel…special to him?

No, it was too much to hope—so she pushed the silly wish from her mind.

Yet even so—despite the pleasures Garon had taught her to share with others, and despite what Garon could probably never feel for her—she drifted into sleep knowing she *was* far more than his slave now, far more than she could have imagined mere weeks earlier.

She was his now, she belonged here, and if nothing ever changed, she would exist here in a state of simple bliss for the rest of her days.

THE MORNING SUN shone down bright as Garon strolled the main street of Myrtell, headed home from the bakery where he'd bought two fresh loaves of bread and some sweet rolls he knew Laela to be particularly fond of.

He'd not been away long, but already he looked forward to seeing his princess. Yes, she could easily stiffen his cock by bathing herself in a wooden tub while he watched—he never got tired of seeing her wet—or by exchanging her soft, lovely touches and kisses with the other girls in the tavern when she was feeling particularly naughty, but it made him just as happy in other ways to simply watch her working about the tavern, to share a meal with her, to simply see her smile.

He burst through the door ready to tempt and tease her with the sweet rolls, to perhaps playfully demand sexual favors in exchange for the sugary treats. It was a game they fell into often, and she would pretend to be very put upon just before she vigorously sucked his cock or wrapped her sumptuous breasts around it.

"Guess what I brought from the baker, princess!" he called, stepping inside.

No one stirred, so he looked in the bedchamber—but all was still there, as well.

Ah, this meant she was at the beach. She seemed continually drawn there—sometimes just for a decadent swim to escape the summer heat and other times for more wet fucking beneath the hot sun. Either way, though, he'd come to enjoy her unlikely love of the ocean, and the sexual aspect had definitely shown him how to enjoy it himself.

Dropping the baked goods on the counter, he headed back out and through the outskirts of the village. Crossing the dunes and the last remains of ancient structures, he thought of her, swimming naked, letting the water sluice over her skin—which was slowly beginning to darken from more time in the sun than she was used to—and his cock lifted slightly. He couldn't quite say why, but he liked the browner skin on her—maybe because it made her seem more like a villager, more like him. And he also liked the wild spirit inside her that led her to swim in the ocean or lick another girl's pussy—the spirit that made her someone who could never really be any man's slave.

As expected, he quickly spotted the mound of green fabric in the sand—but when he looked out to sea, he didn't find her.

He watched for a moment, staring hard, waiting for her head to come bobbing up from under the surface—but still, no Laela.

Dear Ares, where was she?

She couldn't have…drowned, could she? The thought sliced through his heart like a dull knife. "*Laela*," he heard himself utter, feeling helpless.

He shook his head. She couldn't be dead—she just *couldn't*. Maybe she was swimming farther up the shore, carried by the shifting tide. Or maybe she was hiding behind him in the tall dunes, ready to jump out and surprise him. But she couldn't be dead. *Could she?*

He felt faint, weak, at the thought, and dropped to his knees.

Then his gaze fell on *another* bit of green, lying yards away on the beach.

Getting to his feet, he ran toward it…to find the cat's face pendant she wore around her neck. She never took it off—never. Not for swimming. Not for bathing. Not for cleaning. Not for fucking. He grabbed it up from the sand, letting his fist close tight around it.

Laela, my princess, where are you?

That's when he noticed the hoof prints in the sand. Lots of them. Both coming…and going.

Enrick's men.

She'd been taken by Enrick's men.

CHAPTER EIGHT

LAELA LAY RESTING on her old bed, in her old room—someplace she'd never expected to be again. She hugged Midnight to her chest, the cat purring and warm against her as she tried to forget the day just past.

She could scarcely believe her father's men had dragged her back to the fortress naked. It was hard to make herself remember the horror of hearing the hooves, looking up and realizing who bore down upon her, and having no place to run. She'd fought, scratching at skin and eyes—she'd even succeeded in delivering a satisfyingly hard blow to one man's jaw that had knocked him backward onto the sand—but in the end, it hadn't been enough. There had been seven of them and only one of her.

"But my dress!" she'd sobbed—a strange thought, perhaps, given everything else happening, but she'd realized instantly that if she were going to be hauled back to the fortress that she wanted desperately to be covered. Here, in Myrtell, with Garon, she'd grown comfortable with her body, even comfortable with letting others see it—but at the fortress, she was still Laela, the youngest daughter, the little girl, and the freedom she'd felt with Garon would not exist there.

"Forget the dress," said the man who'd hoisted her naked body up onto a horse's back. He'd slapped her bottom, adding, "Let your father see what a little slut you've become."

"Let *everyone* see," another man had said, making the others laugh.

"And what a sight she is," a third fellow had chimed in. She'd closed her eyes by that time, unable to bear keeping them open, unable to watch what befell her. Even so, she'd felt their leering eyes as she'd contemplated the word they used for her—slut. It was a Virg word she'd heard only rarely—a slur for a woman who gave sex freely. No such word existed in Caralonian society, for sex *was* given freely here, an Ares-given gift and right. The insult wounded her, ranking her below other Caralon women—although she'd done nothing other women did not.

"What I wouldn't give for a dip into that royal pussy," another voice added, drawing sounds of lascivious agreement from the others.

"We could each have a turn with her before heading back," someone suggested to her horror.

"And risk Enrick's wrath?"

"Her hair is down, the bride price gone, probably weeks ago. He need never know if we enjoy the tart a bit before returning her."

Tears had threatened, but somehow she'd held them at bay. They wouldn't take her dignity—even if they raped her. Even so, the very notion had paralyzed her, turning her whole body numb with fear. Rape—such an antiquated, barbaric act! How was it that her father's men were so very much like the Virgs? The very idea of rape whisked her thoughts to Garon's mother—and his father. She'd never have dreamed she could be in such danger from anyone in her father's employ—but she supposed her recent actions, added to having been discovered naked just before going for a swim— somehow justified it in their minds.

"I will tell," she'd blurted from her place on the horse.

Their laughter quieted, but the first man, the nearest to her, said, "As if Enrick would believe a word out of your mouth *now*."

"I say he will," she persisted. "And if you rape me, I will look into your eyes the whole time, I will memorize your ugly faces, and I will be able to point my rapists out to my father."

Again, the beach had turned silent other than the shushing tide as the smarmy men weighed her words. Finally, one of them said, "If we really want to fuck the slut, we could do it…and then simply not bring her back. Let her go on her way."

But immediately the head man spoke up. "No. If Enrick ever found out, we'd be dead. Even the ripest piece of ass is not worth that."

And so her heartbeat had calmed a little as the party started back toward the fortress, yet fear of the men had still burned inside her, and they'd continued leering at her with lusty contempt.

Funny, she thought now, she'd never feared Garon that way. Even in the beginning, when he'd made her his slave, when he'd ruled over her sexually, she'd never felt threatened by him. He'd never looked at her with the disrespect her father's men had.

Arriving back at the fort had been the worst humiliation of all. Clearly word of her return had reached her father, for he'd been waiting outside the massive main doors. When she'd been lowered from the horse's back, naked and dirty, she'd instinctively used her hands to cover herself as best she could. Tears had finally come then, at having to face her father that way—and in the company of so many others, too. She'd never known such shame.

"Dear Ares, why has no one covered the girl?" her father boomed, hurriedly stripping off his own large leather vest to wrap about her. Fortunately it hung to her thighs and she instinctively hugged herself to keep it closed in front.

When she managed to meet her father's gaze, she found pain mingled with anger.

"Are you all right?" he asked, voice ragged, his large hands curling into her shoulders.

She nodded shortly.

Next, her father had called for her old maid, Nila, and then Aris. Nila arrived first, her elderly eyes looking worn and worried. "Oh child," she'd gasped at the sight of her.

"Bathe and dress her," Enrick had commanded, "then let her rest."

From there, she'd been rushed here, to her old bedchamber. A bathing tub was brought and filled with cool water—for the day was so hot—and as Nila began to wash her hair, the door opened. Aris came in, Midnight nestled in her arms.

Laela had nearly leapt from the tub. "Midnight!"

Aris smiled at her reaction as Nila said, "Aris here cared for the cat while you were away. Still don't know what a girl needs with a stable cat, but…"

Midnight had let out a hearty meow that seemed to finish the thought.

Now, dressed in a pale blue silk sleeping gown, Laela waited, stroking Midnight's shiny fur. She was supposed to be resting, sleeping, but who could sleep at a time like this? She'd disgraced her family and now she would be forced to face the consequences.

When a knock came on the door, she knew it was her father—he always tried to knock lightly, but had never mastered such softness. She took a deep breath. "Come in."

He entered, his strong face looking drawn, tight. His blue eyes sparkled bright as ever—oh Ares, like Garon's, she realized now for the first time—but his expression remained grim.

She sat up on the bed, pulling Midnight's pliant, furry body into her lap.

"Words cannot describe what you've put me through these past weeks, Daughter," Enrick said, his voice softer than usual, but still wrought with power.

She considered replying, but refrained, sensing he had *much* more to say.

"Worry. Fear. Humiliation. Shame. I've had to watch your mother weep—something you know she doesn't do often—and your sisters worry. It was all their husbands could do to convince them to leave for their homes—otherwise, they'd have waited here forever wondering what became of you.

"You made a fool of me in front of Ogran, a man whose protection is vital to Caralon. You made a fool of *him* before this entire fortress and *his* entire entourage.

"Indeed, your childish actions have reached far and wide, Daughter—so far and so wide that we may not know the ramifications for years to come." He stopped to let out a long sigh. "Have you anything—anything at all—to say for yourself?"

"I am truly sorry, Father. But I simply could not face marrying a man so old. Besides repulsing me, he…frightened me."

She could have sworn a hint of sympathy leaked from her father's eyes, but his voice remained cold as steel. "You are a young girl. Such fears and worries over marriage are normal. That's why there is Orientation."

"It didn't help," she said shortly.

Her father's nostrils flared slightly in dismay and any concern she'd seen in his eyes fled to leave them as cold as his speech. "I have sent a rider to the mountains to summon Ogran, to let him know his bride has been returned. Until his arrival, you are not to leave this chamber."

It felt as if all the air had just been sucked from her lungs. Still? Still, he would marry her to that mean old ogre? And he would hold her captive here in her room until then?

Her back went rigid as she lowered her chin in defiance. She reached out, grabbing onto a lock of the long, loose hair that fell over her shoulder, and spoke forcefully. "Will he still want me once he finds out I no longer possess my bride price?"

Her father's eyes flew wide at the confession. But he kept his response short and sharp. "We will rebraid it. He is old. We can only hope he will not notice."

Laela let out a heavy breath of disgust and disbelief. She wasn't giving up—she was ready to challenge her father head-on. "Maybe I'll tell him. I'll tell him before we even leave here and he won't want me anymore."

"I would tread carefully, Daughter, were I you." His eyes narrowed.

"Or what? What's the worst you can do to me? Give me to Ogran? You're planning on that anyway, so as I see it, I have nothing to lose."

"How could you surrender your bride price?" he

stormed then, raising his arms above his head in outrage. "How in Ares' name did this happen, Daughter? Who did this to you?"

She felt almost as if she physically shrank beneath his ire. She wanted to be brave and fearless, but she'd forgotten how frightening her father could be in his own right. "What does it matter?" she finally said, although she wished the words had come out stronger.

Her father studied her in the stark silence of the room's stone walls, and she knew—Ares forbid—that somehow he'd just seen in her expression that it *did* matter who had taken her bride price. She'd let it leak out through her eyes, or maybe her voice.

His words came quiet but stern. "If I find out who took your virginity, Laela, I will make the man pay."

Now it was she who let *her* eyes narrow on *him*, with hate. She wanted desperately to wound him. "Who says it was only one man?"

Her father gasped, his eyes filled with disappointment.

"Don't act so surprised, Father. You know the way of our world. Only for a royal girl would such an admission earn contempt. I only wish to be normal, to lead a normal life."

But Enrick ignored her pleas, simply replying, "Someone was the first, someone took your bride price, Daughter. And I promise you this. Whether or not the culprit knew who you were and what he was taking— defy me again and I will find him and I will make him very sorry. *You*, on the other hand, will be Ogran's to punish."

With that, he turned and stalked from the room, slamming the heavy wooden door behind him. Laela's heart seemed to pound through her chest, even through her head, it beat so violently. Her stomach shriveled inside her.

Don't cry. Don't cry. As a girl, she'd been the weepiest female she'd ever known, shedding tears at the tiniest event. But now she was a woman, and she would not let silly tears rule her any longer.

Even so, holding them back was difficult when she thought of Garon. Oh, if only she could be back with him in the tavern. Night was falling now, he was likely opening for business. She wanted to be there, serving up ale, giving him hugs and kisses in between passing out goblets to the thirsty men. She wanted to be thrilling him, fucking him. Mostly, she just wanted to *be* with him, in any way she could.

"I hate this place," she murmured to Midnight, tucked cozily at her side. She ran her palm lovingly over the black cat's back. "The only good thing about being back here is you." With that, she hugged the cat tight to her and, listening to him purr, lay wondering what horrors her future held.

GARON'S HEART BEAT wildly against his ribs as he eased into a darkened corridor in Enrick's fortress. Part of him couldn't believe he was actually doing this—he'd never embarked on anything so dangerous in his life and he had no death wish. Yet…how could he not? It hadn't even been a question in his mind. She'd been taken, and he'd had to come for her.

There was no denying it any longer—he cared for her. He cared for her just the way he'd sworn not to do. He'd told himself he didn't want to care because she was trouble and caring would only make it worse, but he knew now that from the first time he'd seen her, he'd felt something, some attraction that went beyond the physical. He'd been fighting with himself and denying it, trying to make it go away ever since—yet he finally had to face the facts—he cared for the girl. More than that. He loved her.

The young man he'd spoken to outside had said to follow the stone corridor until it curved to the left and that the first door would be hers. Again the thought struck him that he must be out of his mind to be sneaking around Enrick's fortress in the middle of the night—yet the moment he found her door, knowing she was behind it, nothing else mattered but getting to her.

Hurrying to reach her, he discovered the door was barred and latched shut from the outside, which meant her father must fear she'd escape again if he didn't lock her in. Quietly removing the barriers, he pushed the wooden door open just enough that he could slip inside.

The room was bathed in darkness other than the patch of moonlight that fell across the foot of the bed.

But it was enough to allow him to see her—his princess—sleeping gently.

The sight froze him in place. He'd never seen her like this before—looking so soft and fresh, a delicate blue gown covering her, her ripe breasts thrusting softly through the fabric, her chestnut locks pulled back in a feminine chignon. Ares, she was beautiful.

He knelt beside her, studied her shut eyelids, her soft lips, listened to her gentle breathing. Then he whispered, "Princess. Princess, wake up." He lowered a tender touch to her shoulder, hoping not to frighten her.

Her eyes opened, then grew round and wide on him. She bolted upright, throwing her arms around his neck. "Garon! What in Ares' name are you doing here?"

Ah, but it felt good to hold her, sending a burst of warmth radiating through his body from head to toe. Finally, he pulled back to look at her. "I had to find you, Laela."

She shook her head, appearing baffled. "But how…?"

"Once you mentioned to me a boy, a guard named Donnell—do you remember?"

She nodded.

"You said he was a good sort, that he'd let you leave on the night you ran away, so I figured he was my best chance. I found him and explained that you had been with me since you left the fortress. He let me pass without making the other guards aware and he told me how to find you."

"But…why? Why did you come?"

"I brought you this," he said, ignoring her question for the moment to reach in a pocket on his leather vest and pull out her cat pendant.

She gasped softly when she saw it, then lifted her gaze to his. "Thank you, Garon."

"I know you cherish it."

"Yes," she said, taking it from his hand and clutching it close to her heart. Only then she peered back up at him, her eyes worried. "But…you didn't risk your life to bring this to me. So…why?"

"I've come to steal you away," he replied, then tried for a grin. "You are my slave, after all. I'm only taking back what's mine."

She didn't return the smile. "No," she said, "I cannot go with you. If we were caught, you would be killed."

Somehow, that threat had never quite been enough to keep him away from Laela. And, oddly, now that the threat was more imminent, it mattered less than ever. "I don't care."

She pursed her lips, her expression adamant. "I won't go with you, Garon. I can't."

"Why not?"

"*You* may not care if you die, but *I* do." Her hazel eyes went soft, sad, more vulnerable than he'd ever seen them, just before she lowered them to his chest. "I…I love you."

The words were like a balm to a wound he'd never before realized he possessed. They covered him like a protective blanket—and made him fearless. Fearless of

Enrick, and fearless of his *own*emotions, too. "I love you, too, princess. Why else would I be here?"

Laela felt faint beneath the weight of his unexpected words. Had he really just told her he loved her—the same as she loved him? It seemed like an impossible dream come true.

Slowly, she lifted her gaze to his blue, blue eyes, and in that moment, she knew they were *hers*. That everything inside him was *hers*. To love. To cherish. To own forever.

Unable to help herself, she wrapped her arms around him and relished the warmth of his hard body pressed close against her curves. She'd thought she'd never have this again and her breasts ached with need, her pussy wept with want of him.

She knew she wasn't alone in her desire when his strong hand rose to her breast, first just cupping the side, then molding her, reshaping her in his palm to send a hot blast of desire exploding through her like a shooting star in the night sky.

"I need you," she said low in his ear.

He crushed her breast more tightly in his hand and she felt the wrenching need moving through him, as well.

"I must have you," she breathed, then reached to press her palm over his shaft. It stretched long and thick and hard against her touch, making her cunt throb with the emptiness of not having him inside her. "Fill me," she whispered, drawing him onto the bed with her.

A small growl left him as his eyes fell half shut with a steamy lust she wanted to slake. She worked at the lacings of his pants as he reached for the long hem of her sleeping gown, sliding his hand up her inner thigh and directly onto her swollen mound. His fingers dipped into her moisture on contact, rapidly stroking, stroking, making her pant with the quick waves of pleasure now washing over her.

"So wet for me, princess. Your pussy is always so wet."

At that moment, she finished her struggle with his pants and his handsome, hungry cock burst free. "Oh!" she said at the very sight of it. It had only been last night that she'd last seen it, but having thought it was gone from her...she'd never witnessed a lovelier sight. "Fuck me, Garon," she pleaded. "Fuck me hard."

His eyes darkened at her command as his fingers pushed up inside her cunt, now pulsing for him. He thrust them deep, hard, and she drank in the promise they made. "Yes, yes," she said in a low rasp, meeting his dangerous gaze, hoping he saw how very much she wanted him to command her, control her, take her.

His fingers plunged, plunged, and she stroked his length in the same rhythm until they were both breathing heavy, eyes locked, bodies primed for more. "Don't make me wait, Garon. I long for your cock. I must have it deep inside me or I'll die."

At that, he braced his hands on her shoulders and pushed down on the bed, pinning her there, hovering over her, his eyes still issuing the most delicious threat. Wild with want, she parted her legs as wide as possible, opening herself to everything he had to give. He glanced down at her open folds in the moonlit room, let out a low, hot groan, then thrust himself deep inside, to the hilt, making them both let out deep cries of satisfaction.

Her first inclination was to hold him tight, just feel him next to her, inside her—but she didn't get the chance before he began to deliver deep, pounding strokes that reached her very core. There was nothing but *him* in that moment, filling her up, making of her something new, raising her to an entirely new plane. She lifted her hips to meet every hot plunge and take him into her as far as possible.

"I want to make you come," he growled, his breath hot, his eyes like that of a ferocious animal.

And with that, he rolled them both in the bed without ever letting their bodies part, until he lay on his back and she straddled his hips. "Oh!" she cried at the deeper sense of impact.

And then her body took over. There was no thought, only the sensual grind, the physical abandon that led her up, up, toward that sweetest of peaks.

Her blue gown pooled around them both, but Garon kneaded her breasts through the thin fabric, fueling her fevered desire. He pinched her nipples, squeezed the ample flesh around them, stroked strong thumbs over the jutting points in such a way that the silk between them added to the sizzle of friction there. "More," she pleaded.

She had no idea how he could know exactly what she wanted just from that one word, but he did. Pulling the string above her breasts, the fabric loosened until he drew it from her shoulders, freeing her breasts. She leaned over him, loving the way his mouth opened, waiting for her to lower her beaded nipple. As his lips closed over the turgid peak, she said, "Suck me hard," and he did, in rhythm with her movements, the hot strokes pushing her higher, higher. The pleasure echoed through breasts and pussy, taking her over, drowning any other thought but that of orgasm.

And then it broke—hot and hard and overwhelming because this time she knew it was filled with love. "I love you, Garon, I love you," she cried as the heat radiated through her in those hot, delectable waves. "I love you!"

"I want you in a new way now, princess," he said from below her, his voice dark, low.

Something in the suggestion made her lips tremble. She should have been worried about a hundred other things—like someone finding him here, like her impending marriage to Ogran—yet the shadowy quality in his words made her wonder, whatever new he had in mind for her, could she bear it? Would she love it? Surely, if Garon wanted it, she would—yet what if she did not? "What new way?" she whispered.

He pulled her down close, their bodies still connected, and whispered hotly in her ear. "I want to put my cock in your perfect little ass."

She drew in her breath as her pussy seized with desire. She knew his fingers, in that area, had brought her great pleasure, and she remembered once, in the very beginning, that Baelor had mentioned Garon fucking her ass—but what would that be like? "Will…will it fit?"

She felt his smile more than saw it. "I will *make* it fit, Laela. And you will scream with pleasure, so loud that we will give thanks these walls are made of stone." He chuckled in her ear and she returned the giggle, suddenly anxious to try, anxious to experience what he wanted to give her.

"Do it," she said warmly. "Fuck my ass."

She rolled off of him in the bed and he positioned himself behind her, kneeling between her parted knees. "Oh Laela," he said, kneading her bare bottom, her gown in a crush of silk at her waist now. "So pretty, so round."

She lay on her belly, head propped on her stacked hands, and licked her lip as the sensation of his touch in that sensitive region—as well as the vision in her head of what he saw and how much he seemed to like it—amplified her passion. On impulse, she arched her ass a bit higher for him, making him groan.

And then came his finger, stroking the fissure there, stroking, stroking, making her sigh with unimaginable pleasure. "Oh, I could come just from that," she said, wondering if she really could.

He gave a low, heated laugh. "Maybe you will before it's done, princess."

With that, he dipped the tip of one finger inside, making her cry out, then smoothly slid it deeper.

The insertion forced her to pull in her breath at the unusual pleasure it delivered. She bit her lip, trying to grow accustomed to it, then soaking it in, simply enjoying. "Oh—oh Garon, I truly think I will. I truly think I shall come like this."

Another dark chuckle sounded behind her as he bent to lower a soft, sensual bite to her shoulder. "You are delectable, my princess."

The sentiment ran through her like a warm, thick drink. "Fuck me now, Garon. Fuck my ass. Show me what it feels like."

She didn't complain, however, when he didn't extract his finger right away. For instead, he began to move it in and out vigorously, making her sob and moan with the dark pleasure. She moved against it, meeting the thrusts, unwittingly rubbing her mound against the fur bedcovering at the same time. "Oh Garon," she purred, caught up in the delight. "Yes, Garon, so good."

"More now, princess," he said, his voice deep as the night as he withdrew his finger and pressed the tip of his cock to her anus.

"Oh!" Just *that* was amazing. Logistically, it seemed impossible for his tremendous shaft to enter her there, but at the same time, she wanted this desperately. "More, my lover, more."

He answered by pushing, prodding. It stretched her painfully and she let out a cry of distress, but added just as quickly, "Don't stop. I need you there. Keep going." She remembered another time when a burst of pain had led to the most delicious of pleasures.

He didn't reply, but she heard his heavy breath at her back, felt the incredible pressure of his rhythmic pushes against that tiny opening. She tried to focus on relaxing, both her mind and her body, so that her flesh would welcome him. And for a brief time, truly, it felt as if her body was being split apart by the power of his rigid cock, but then slowly, slowly, the fissure began to respond and he pushed slightly inside.

"Oh yes!" she cried, shocked at the sensation. So full, tight. Amazing and strange.

But he wasn't done yet, pushing more, stretching her farther and farther—long moments of gritting her teeth through a pain that was pleasure and a pleasure that was pain—until suddenly his cock slid deep, sinking home, filling her impossibly full.

"Oh Ares! Oh!"

His hands closed firm on her bare arms as his chest warmed her back. "I am in your ass now, princess. Deep inside you."

She pulled in her breath, let it back out, tried to breathe normally. But the sensation was overwhelming. Despite the summer heat, cold chills ran the length of her body at a union she might have once imagined impossible, maybe even *forbidden* in some way—yet now she knew it was the most fitting thing in the world to interlock her body with Garon's in yet another amazing way.

She'd gone still to let him enter her, but now she

slowly, instinctively lifted against him.

He groaned. "Ares, yes."

Very gently, he began to move, pulling out just a little, then pushing back in. The moan that left her came from deep inside. And when she met the slow thrusts, her clit brushed against the fur underneath her.

Each of Garon's strokes came a little longer than the last, a little firmer. She'd never felt so thoroughly penetrated by him before, so very under his control, and so very overwhelmed by the sheer power of it. She clenched her teeth in a hard pleasure that became the biggest part of her. That pleasure seemed to vibrate outward—not only through her pussy and breasts, but to the tips of her fingers and toes, even pulsing through her neck and head. Faster and faster he thrust, and she met each, driving her ass back against him—for there was no more pain now, only deep enveloping pleasure.

Still harder and more intensely he pummeled her—until a bit of pain returned, but it was good, so good. She wanted all of it, everything he had to give.

She cried out, suffering sensation everywhere, letting it consume her. Nothing existed outside of this room, even outside of her body. She closed her eyes, saw swirling colors, clawed her fingers into the fur, met his strokes, met them hard, and in between each let her pussy brush teasingly against the fur bedcovering.

Pleasure came from every direction, even more when his hands dug beneath her, cupping her breasts, her sensitive nipples catching between his fingers.

Fuck me. Fuck me. Fuck me. The thought pounded through her with each stroke, but she could no longer form words. She sobbed. Screamed. Too much pleasure. How could she take any more? His big cock so tight in her ass, her pussy rubbing so hard now, insistent, against the bed. *Fuck me. Fuck me.*

And then—oh! Sweet, hot orgasm. Bursting over her. Drowning her in the heat, in the impossible pleasure. She screamed her ecstasy, over and over, until behind her Garon groaned, "Ares, I'm coming, princess! I'm coming in your ass!"

Brutal strokes connected with her nether regions as he spilled his seed inside her, and then they went still, both exhausted, Laela nearly forgetting where she was, *who* she was.

Until she glanced up at the window. The *open* window, letting the moonlight pour over them. "Garon," she said quickly. "The window. It's open."

He still lay atop her, inside her. "Mmm."

"I've been screaming," she reminded him.

He only chuckled, lost in post-orgasmic peace. "Just as I promised."

"Someone surely heard. Especially toward the end. I was so loud."

Behind her, his body tensed as he finally understood. "Ares," he bit off.

"You have to get out of here."

"Come with me, Laela," he pleaded, hurriedly rising off of her, leaving her ass to feel oddly ajar as he pulled out.

She ignored the strange sensation and rolled to her back. "No, Garon, I can't! I can't risk being caught with you. He'll kill you! Now go! Before it's too late!"

His eyes went steely as he stepped into the thick shaft of moonlight. "Then I'll be back."

Sitting up, she punched one fist into the bed next to her. "No! You will be put to death and I couldn't bear it."

"*I* cannot bear the idea of you married to some old man who will not cherish you as you should be!"

Outside, she heard the sounds of men walking, shuffling. "Came from this way," someone said. Drat it all—they *had* heard!

Thrusting her arms back into the short sleeves of her sleeping gown, she leapt from the bed and grabbed Garon's wrist, dragging him to the door. "Don't come again—it's too dangerous!"

"Meet me," he insisted.

"What?"

"Tomorrow night, in the breezeway with the white columns. Donnell said it was the easiest way in, so it's also the easiest way out."

She pulled in her breath impatiently. Time was too short for this. "But I'm locked in this room."

"You cannot get someone to let you out?"

She sighed, still trying to rush him along. "Maybe."

"If you are not there at midnight, I'll come back *here*, to your room."

"No, Garon."

"We'll escape the fortress grounds and then we can be together."

"But they will find me. Myrtell is too close."

"You're right. We'll leave Myrtell."

"Fine, then. Now go! Hurry. All that matters now is getting you out of here before it's too late. And you must re-latch my door!"

Her last glimpse of him held sparkling blue eyes and his usual wicked smile. "I'll see you at midnight, princess."

As she heard him bar the door behind him, Laela nearly pounced into bed, reaching to retie the front of her gown. Moments later, the door burst back open and her father rushed in, followed by two guards, each carrying a torch. "Laela!"

She shot upright, trying to look frightened—which wasn't difficult under the circumstances. "What? What's going on?"

Her father's expression shone grim with concern. "The guards said they heard screams coming from the direction of your window."

She hoped the glow of sex didn't shimmer on her face, or that the smell of intimacy didn't hang in the air. "Perhaps I was having a nightmare," she replied pointedly. "A nightmare of being dragged off to the mountains with an old man."

She let her gaze pierce her father's coldly, but inside she still basked in the pleasure that had been far more like a dream than a nightmare. Garon had come for her! Garon loved her!

She wished she could have left with him, but she refused to risk his life that way. And as for tomorrow night, well—she'd deal with that then. For now, his love would be enough to keep her going.

CHAPTER NINE

THE NEXT DAY, as Laela somberly ate lunch in the great hall with her mother, father and many of the fortresses employees, a messenger came bounding in the huge main door of the fort. "Enrick, I come with news."

Her father lowered his goblet to the table and said, "Share it then."

"A rider tells us Ogran's caravan has been spotted in the hills directly to the west, and estimates they will arrive sometime tomorrow."

The words sent a shiver down Laela's spine. Last night with Garon had been so all-consumingly wonderful that she'd somehow managed not to let herself think about the ugly reality of Ogran much since then. But tomorrow would come quickly.

In that moment, she wished she *had* left with Garon—perhaps if they'd departed as soon as he'd awakened her, they could have indeed escaped without being seen. Especially if Donnell was willing to help.

However, another ugly reality loomed, too—the

opposite outcome. Leaving this place with Garon would mean risking his very life, and how could she possibly do that? She loved him, and she'd rather live a hideous existence with Ogran than see her lover put to death. And maybe Aris was right—maybe Ogran would die soon, and then she and Garon could be together. Yet…that hardly seemed a good answer to such an impossible dilemma.

"Very well," Enrick said, then shifted his gaze to his daughter. "Tomorrow you will be given to Ogran. Do not disappoint me as you did before."

"How could I? You have me locked in my room."

Her father's brow narrowed in anger. "I meant that I expect you to treat Ogran with fitting respect when he arrives."

Despite her better judgment, she couldn't resist rolling her eyes. "An old man who takes a young girl for a wife against her will deserves little respect in my opinion."

Enrick slammed his fist down on the table, making all the plates and goblets flinch against the wood. Everyone froze in place. "Go to your bedchamber, now," he commanded her. "I thought perhaps you could behave in a civilized enough manner to be out among us today. I had hoped perhaps we could put your recent bad decisions behind us. But I see my hopes were misplaced. You shall remain in your room until the Giving Ceremony."

Laela glanced at her mother. Jalal's eyes brimmed

with distress, but she didn't intercede. Which meant once again, Laela was on her own to save herself. Unless…there *was* someone who might be able to help her. She glanced toward her old teacher and Orienter, Aris, seated further down the table. "Might Aris come with me, Father?"

"What for?" he boomed.

She answered just as sharply, refusing to cower beneath his tone. "I am to be given over for marriage tomorrow and I did not get to finish my Orientation—*that's* what for."

Enrick waved his hand absently through the air. "Fine then. Fine. Aris, you may go. Just see that she gets to the room, and see that she is properly locked in when you leave."

"Of course," Aris answered, keeping her voice quiet, her eyes down.

However, as soon as the two women had exited the great hall for the privacy of a stone corridor, Laela stopped and grabbed onto Aris' wrist. "Aris, I need your help."

LATE THAT NIGHT, Aris enclosed Laela in a warm embrace, lowering a soft kiss on her lips that spoke of encouragement, bravery and maybe even goodbye. Then the teacher slipped out the door and conveniently forgot to latch it.

Laela had not yet decided if she was going to attempt

an escape with Garon, for she remained torn, unsure she could live without him, but also knowing she couldn't live with *herself* if she caused his death. If he were to be found on the grounds by himself, well, then he was an intruder of some sort, a thief, and would be punished accordingly—but probably not severely. Yet if he were to be found with *her*...it was unthinkable.

The one thing she *did* know, however, was that she could not leave him in the breezeway at midnight, wondering where she was and why she hadn't come. She also couldn't let him put himself at further risk by sneaking deeper into the fortress as he had last night.

As evidence of just how undecided she remained, when she left her chamber, she carried a sack containing a skirt, tunic and a few other belongings—yet she went to meet him still in the same white sleeping gown she'd put on hours earlier. Stay or go? She simply didn't know the answer.

Just as she stepped free from the enclosed stone corridor to the covered walkway supported by thick whitewashed columns, a light wind cooled her face and lifted her tresses—and she saw Garon.

A lock of warm blond hair fell waywardly over his forehead. His dark leather vest revealed the tanned, well-muscled arms of a hardworking man. His blue eyes spoke of grim determination...and passion. It struck her how different he looked than the first time she'd seen him—when his expression had been easy, light, uncaring—and she couldn't help but think she had changed him. She had made him into the passionate man who stood before her now. Her breasts ached and her cunt spasmed softly at the mere knowledge.

Yet it was in that moment she knew the answer to her dilemma. He was too beautiful to risk—no matter how great the gain. "I…cannot go with you," she said softly, padding toward him. The night breeze wafting in from the coast lifted her hair once more and left the fabric of her gown fluttering in soft waves behind her.

His expression darkened accordingly. "Laela, you must."

Upon reaching him, she lifted her hands to his broad chest, bare beneath the vest and sprinkled with light curls. "Garon, I simply cannot risk you. I love you too much."

As he folded her in his arms, he leaned in close to whisper near her ear. "That's sweet, princess, but I'm not afraid."

She let out a sigh, pulling back. "Yet *I* am, don't you see? I could never forgive myself if I caused your death."

His firm grip closed around her elbows. "And I would never forgive *myself* if I let you be taken off by some crusty old man who will mistreat you." Then he lowered his gaze, looking almost ashamed. "Yet…maybe I am just as guilty of that."

Laela shook her head vehemently. "No, never. I *wanted* the things you wanted. I wanted them because it pleased me to please you. It pleased me more than I knew was possible." She reached up to touch his stubbled cheek and he raised his gaze back to hers. She looked deeply into his eyes and prayed to Ares that he could feel her next words as profoundly as she did. "Garon, being your slave set me free."

After a long moment of silence, when only their eyes spoke of all they had shared, he said softly, "I *could* remind you that you *are* my slave. I could demand that you leave with me."

Her words sounded just as calm and certain. "But you won't. Because you never made me do anything that felt wrong to me, and I know you won't start now."

He let out a sigh, his gaze going weary. "So I am supposed to just leave you here, just let your father marry you to an old man who will take you far, far away. I am supposed to let you be forced into a terrible life you don't desire and do nothing to stop it?"

His determination to save her was no less than breathtaking, yet... "We *tried* to stop it. You tried to help me. You *did* help me—more than you know. Because of you, I will always have wonderful, thrilling, *loving* memories. It's...more than I could have hoped or dreamed."

Garon's hands rose to bracket her face just before he melded his mouth to hers in a powerful kiss that moved through her like bottled lightning. Drawing near, she couldn't ignore the pleasure of his erection, pressing hot and hard into her most tender, hungry place. She moved against him, almost involuntarily, needing more—he was impossible to resist.

Oh, how she longed to have him inside her—the thick need pulsed through her, something she couldn't even begin to push down. She eased her hand between them, pressing her palm against the solid rock between his thighs, needing to touch him there.

Without planning it, her other hand came between them, too, her fingers pulling at the lacings that stretched over his powerful shaft. Pulling, clawing—she had to get them undone.

"What are you doing?" he asked on a heavy breath between kisses.

Her own voice came labored. "I won't send you away like this." Finally, she was able to spread the leather, to reach between and wrap her hand full around his wonderful hardness. "One last time," she said.

She watched as he drew in his breath, his look a familiar one of fire—yet… "It isn't safe," he said, flicking his glance briefly into the darkness around them on both sides of the breezeway.

Stark fear and realization shot through her like an arrow to her heart. "Oh Ares, you're right. What am I thinking?" This man literally stole her good sense away.

Pulling back, she looked into those heated eyes that had thrilled her, comforted her, loved her—and had never once frightened her. She lifted a soft kiss to his mouth with lips left swollen from a more brutal meeting just a moment ago, then squeezed his hand and turned to leave her love behind.

But just as quickly, he grabbed onto her wrist and

hauled her back against him, hard. "What you're thinking, princess," he said, his voice as dark as their desire, "is what *I'm* thinking. That the danger is worth it."

Laela sucked in her breath at the truth in his words, then did what she couldn't *not* do, what her body led her to do, what her soul insisted upon. She dropped to her knees.

His eyes, above her, were fraught with too many emotions to name. And as she ran both palms up his majestic cock, finally cradling the head gently in her hands, she realized that the danger with him had *always* been worth it. *Always*.

And especially now.

If we are to part forever, let us have this.

Taking him in her hand, she lowered her mouth firmly onto the hot column of flesh that jutted so prominently toward her. She could tell he tried to hold his groan inside, but he failed, and she couldn't push down the hint of feminine satisfaction that flickered through her.

He was so big in her mouth, filling it so well. She wanted to pleasure him as she'd never wanted before. She wanted to feel the power of him this way one last time, wanted to remind herself that she was his oh-so-willing slave, serving him, exciting him, taking him to heaven on earth.

His fingers threaded through her hair, held it back from her face, massaged her scalp. She felt his eyes burning into her from above, studying her every move, watching her worship him, and the knowledge sent ripples of sensation through her pussy.

"You suck me so good, princess," he whispered, low and raspy. "Nothing feels better on me than your mouth…sucking, sucking. Except maybe…"

Still sliding her widely stretched lips up and down his sturdy length, she gazed up at him.

He cast his classic wicked grin. "Except maybe your sweet, tight little cunt."

With that, he reached for her shoulders, urging her off his cock, to her feet. Her mouth felt pleasantly swollen yet empty upon releasing him, and she hoped he could somehow see how stretched and widened her lips were because of him filling them so well.

"Turn around," he said when their eyes met.

She didn't argue, lost to him now, lost to their sex.

"Brace your arms against the column," he said as she faced away from him, so she pressed her palms flush against the wooden support, and when she felt her gown whisper quickly up her thighs, his hands following, skimming lightly up her skin until they curved over her ass, she instinctively arched toward him.

His hands kneaded her softness there, massaging hard and deep in a way that reached to the core of her desire, and then he kneeled to kiss the soft flesh of her ass, and lower, lower. She arched more, parted her legs— her pussy felt engorged beyond recognition, like it must be the biggest part of her. It pulsed with a need she'd never known as her panting breath filtered into the night air.

She gasped when Garon's mouth sank home at her cunt and she spread her legs even wider, wider, wanting to give her whole self to him there in the breezeway. Licks, kisses, teeth, tongue—she practically clawed at the column that supported her, moaning from the attention at her pussy. Pressure, glorious pressure from both hands and mouth, prodding, invading, pushing into her, parting her folds, making her wide and open for him, for all he wanted to give.

"Fuck me," she heard herself whisper without planning. For his hands and mouth were delectable, but she needed something deeper—and harder, too. She needed his stiff cock inside her.

He rose behind her, his leather leggings pressing warm into her bare skin, his erection nestling hard in the valley of her ass. His hands dug into the flesh of her hips and she thrust back against him, silently begging for what she needed.

"Sweet princess," he murmured just before she felt his hot shaft nudging at her pussy, and then the hard, deep plunge that drew a cry from her throat as overwhelming pleasure spread through her every limb.

"Oh! Oh, you're in me!" she sobbed heatedly over her shoulder.

"Deep inside your hot little cunt," he murmured raspily near her ear.

"Fuck me, Garon. Hard."

He growled at the demand and wasted no time in delivering hard, pummeling strokes that jolted her body and sent hot pleasure flaring through her entire being. Nothing else existed but his cock inside her pussy, connecting their bodies, connecting their souls. Time stood still as she clutched at the wide beam in front of her, so happily taking each punishing drive he delivered.

"So wet," he murmured, his breath warm in her ear. "So wet and hot for me, princess."

"Just for you," she sighed. "Only for you."

His hand slid smoothly around the front of her thigh, sinking between, his fingers quickly finding her clit. The moan that left her was deep, coming someplace low and buried inside her. "Yes," she whispered.

Two roughened fingers rubbed delicious circles over the needy, distended nub as he continued his hard strokes from behind. Now Laela practically hugged the column, weak from the heated delight but determined to see it through to the end. "Oh Ares," she moaned softly. "Oh Ares, yes."

She took his pleasure from both sides, stunned, amazed, lost, eyes peering up beyond the wooden awning over the breezeway to the brilliant stars dotting the black sky. She drank in each of Garon's hot thrusts, moved against his generous, skilled fingers, and almost as quickly as she knew she was going to come, it was happening—she was still staring heavenward, but now soaring through the night sky as if her body had been shot up, up, up, and she sobbed, high and soft, at each delicious pulsation.

Then she found herself back in his arms and they were sinking, toward the ground, because her knees were giving way. But Garon was there with her for every inch of the soft descent, his arms anchored at her waist, and the next thing she knew, they were on their knees on the cool, smooth stone, still fucking, hard slow strokes, hard, hard, each echoing through her like a reminder of his love, until he breathed, "Ares, yes," emptying his hot fluids deep inside her accepting body.

They stayed that way, him hunched low over her back, for a long silent moment of recovery. Silent, but Laela's mind began to spin.

What she'd just experienced with him was the most incredible experience of her life. The danger *was* always worth it. *Maybe he's right, maybe I should leave with him.*

As if reading her thoughts, he said, "Come with me."

It seemed simple at moments, like this, like there was no other choice. But what if…what if they were caught? What if he died?

"Your friend Donnell will help us. He let me in again tonight. He will help us leave the grounds undetected."

Laela's breath grew thick, her chest heaving, as she turned toward him, both of them kneeling, and took his hands. There *was* no other choice. They *could* escape. Donnell would help them and Ares would guide them, and they could have it *all*. All happiness, more happiness than she could even fathom.

She was just about to say yes when a gruff voice cut into her thoughts. "Over there! Shine the torch!"

Laela and Garon both looked up as firelight lit their faces in shock. Everything inside Laela froze in pure terror as her father's men closed in on them, the guards seeming to come from every direction.

"Summon Enrick from his bed!" someone yelled.

"He is on his way already," another voice answered.

Laela clutched helplessly at Garon, who pulled her into a hard, desperate embrace, warm against his strong chest. She caught a glimpse of Donnell standing behind some other men, his expression one of sorrow and apology, and she knew this had not been his fault—she and Garon had simply taken too big of a risk.

It occurred to her, though, that maybe since she had *his* sympathy, perhaps she could earn it from others, too. Not the men who'd dragged her from the beach—for she saw their faces among those around her—but there were so many others, probably fifteen or twenty men now made a circle around them.

"Let him go," she beseeched them. "He's done no wrong but to care for me. Please let him go before my father comes—please save his life."

Some of the men's faces around her did fill with pity then, maybe indecision, but no one made a move or said a word in favor of setting Garon free.

"Please," she begged again, turning from his arms and folding her hands together as if in prayer. "Please let him live."

Still, no one moved, even as eyes darkened in regret around her.

Tears rolled down her cheeks by the time her father's imposing figure appeared, towering above the guards. "What in Ares' name..." he began, ire shining in his eyes as he glared down to where she knelt. Then his gaze drifted behind her, to Garon.

"We heard noises coming from this direction, Enrick." The voice, brutal and familiar, drew her eyes to the man from the beach who'd refused to let her dress, and who'd been the most eager to see her suffer. "Noises of fucking," he said bluntly, his expression filled with disdain as he looked on her as if she were a bit of dirt on his boot.

"Father, please," she begged, still in a position of prayer, tears streaming down both her cheeks now, "please don't hurt him. His only crime is to care for me."

Yet her father's face—once filled with such love and compassion for her—had already turned to stone. He didn't look at her when he said, "This man shall be put to death tomorrow. Chain him in the stables and stand guard over him until such time as I arrange for his execution."

Stark panic shot through Laela like a blow to the stomach and she lunged into Garon's arms, desperate to protect him. They closed around her, so tight she couldn't be sure who was protecting whom—but soon the two of them were being pulled apart, even as she cried, "No! Please, no! I beg of you! Please don't hurt him!"

And Garon's eyes reached out to her, full of love, as he said, "Don't worry for me, princess. I have no regrets. No regrets."

Guards' hands encircled her arms, holding her back, as she watched in horror while chains were tightened around Garon's wrists and ankles, the horrible clanging, clanking sound of them seeming to mock her.

"I love you," she cried through her tears.

"I love you, too, my princess." Their eyes met and his seemed to reach out to her. "Listen to me. Forget about this. Forget about me. Live your life."

She simply looked at him, knowing it was the most impossible request anyone had ever made of her, and she didn't answer, for she also knew her gaze spoke her feelings loud and clear.

His relayed emotion, as well. They both knew she would never recover from this.

CHAPTER TEN

L AELA DIDN'T SLEEP that night. She wondered if she would ever sleep again.

Guilt pummeled her as mightily as Garon's cock had hours before. Oh, how selfish she'd been, how careless, to think that having him one last time would be all right, to think the danger was worth it. Now, because of her and her silly physical desires, he would die. He would be no more. "Oh Garon," she sobbed into the fur bedcovering as she hugged Midnight to her side. Then she reached up to touch the cat pendant at her throat.

She'd put it back on as soon as he'd departed her bedchamber the previous night. Her mother had given her the pendant—but Garon had brought it back to her because he knew she cherished it. Now it would always feel like a gift from *him*.

She never should have run away. If she'd never run away, if she'd just accepted her fate—no matter how awful—none of this would ever have happened, and Garon would be living a happy, peaceful life at the tavern. She'd taken feminine pride in making him care, in turning him from a harder, rougher man into one with softness and love in his eyes—but what she wouldn't give now to change all that, to know he was still living his carefree existence in Myrtell, where his biggest problems had been how much ale to stock and which woman to bed.

"I'm so sorry, Garon," she said helplessly toward the stone ceiling of her room. "I never meant to hurt you."

She clutched again at the cat pendant, then departed the bed for the window. The same stars she'd looked at while they'd fucked still shone above, yet now they seemed cold and distant. "Oh Ares," she prayed aloud, "please save him. Please save the man I love."

SHE MUST HAVE drifted off to sleep, for the sun shone in her window when Nila woke her.

As soon as the events of the night before entered her mind, she bolted upright, grabbing Nila's soft old hands in hers. "Tell me he's not dead yet, Nila! Tell me it's not too late!"

"Shhh now," Nila said, running a soothing hand back through Laela's hair. "He is yet alive. And now your mother summons you."

"My mother?" Jalal had been disappointingly silent on all matters concerning her youngest daughter's fate since the moment Enrick had announced she was to marry Ogran, so this news surprised Laela.

Nila nodded. "She awaits you in the great hall, and I understand she's summoned your father, too."

Laela caught her breath and dressed quickly, with Nila's help, in a pale leather skirt and matching vest.

When she entered the great hall, all lay still and silent, her parents not at their thrones but sitting at the large dining table where they took their meals. A tray of cheeses and fruits had been laid out, but Laela had no appetite. She made eye contact with her mother as she approached, but ignored her father completely. She didn't know him anymore.

"It would appear we are all here now, Wife," Enrick said, sounding irritated. "So now you may say why you called us here."

Jalal pushed to her feet, wearing her usual signature sky blue silk, and looking as strong and powerful as Laela had ever seen her. She addressed her husband pointedly. "If this man, Garon, loves our daughter enough to risk his life for her, does that not matter to you?"

"In what way did he risk—"

Jalal cut him off soundly. "The man came here knowing full well his fate if he was caught. I can scarcely think of any greater risk a person could take."

"Even so, he defiled our daughter, taking her bride price and—"

His wife interrupted him once more. "Husband, I have never interfered with your decisions for our daughters, even when I have had to bite my tongue to stay quiet, but now I must. And I beseech you, Enrick. I beseech you to look into your heart and remember love."

"Jalal, sit down this instant," he snapped.

She ignored the command, but let her voice soften. "Enrick, do you not remember when you and I met—the night we spent in your tent, the way you loved me even though it made no sense, even though there was adversity?"

"What in Ares name does *that* have to do with *this*?"

"It has *everything* to do with this, husband. For I have been to the stables this morning." Enrick's eyes blazed with anger, but Jalal continued, clearly undaunted, as Laela watched in shock. "I have visited with Garon, talked with him, and I see that *same* love in his eyes for our Laela." She paused, took a deep breath, and perhaps waited for Enrick to argue, but for once, he stayed quiet. "Let her be happy, Enrick. It is not so much to ask."

Her mother's words delivered the first bit of real hope Laela had felt since being captured on the beach. Although when Jalal finished, a hard tension grew in the room, something Laela could feel gathering around them like a storm—until finally her father pushed to his feet and spewed the ire Laela had grown to expect from him lately. "I have committed her to another. It is that simple!"

"Fine, I will marry Ogran," Laela announced, standing up as well. "But in exchange for that, let Garon go free!"

Her father's eyes narrowed on her and she knew he was seething with an anger too great to measure, at being defied by them both. He spoke through clenched teeth. "Perhaps, before, when you ran away, this Garon didn't knowingly commit a crime against this house—but last night, he *did*. He came here to take you away when he knows you are a royal daughter promised to another! He will take his just punishment, Laela, and nothing you can do will stop it." With that, Enrick stalked from the table and out of the hall, Laela and Jalal watching helplessly behind him.

Sinking back into familiar despair, Laela went instinctively to her mother's arms, where she collapsed in the tears she'd sworn she wouldn't cry any more.

LATER THAT DAY, Laela was notified by Nila that Ogran had arrived. "You're to come to the lawn dressed in something befitting your position, your father says," she relayed, then proceeded to dress Laela in a silk dress the color of a peach.

"I am to be put on display for that old man," she said glumly as Nila brushed her hair. "Are you going to rebraid it?" she asked over her shoulder then, turning from the viewing glass before her.

Nila shook her head. "Your father did not say to."

Laela gave a short nod. "He had spoken of lying to the old man about my bride price. Perhaps he's come to his senses on at least *that* point." She couldn't help thinking, too, with fleeting hope, that perhaps Ogran would not want her once it was clear she was no longer a virgin—he'd seemed to prize that particular trait so deeply. Yet then again—perhaps he would simply punish her for it in some way.

She suppressed a small shiver, realizing she had to be brave and face the day. Her only thoughts of sadness were for Garon—whatever happened to *her* she could handle. It was knowing and fearing his doom that broke her heart now.

When Laela proceeded down the breezeway—light and sunny beneath a blue sky, the whitewashed columns shining brightly—all eyes on the lawn turned toward her. A huge crowd had gathered, and at its center stood her father, her mother and the grizzly Ogran, who she could not even bear to look at. She lowered her eyes immediately upon catching sight of him, even as her heartbeat kicked up.

Then it struck her. *Was this the Giving Ceremony?* And she was to be sent off with him *now, today,* without knowing for sure what happened to Garon?

But then, maybe it was better this way. Maybe she'd be happier if she never knew for sure—if she could always keep a shred of hope alive by wondering if perhaps he'd managed to get free somehow.

"My daughter, Laela," Enrick said, presenting her as she made her way to the center of the crowd.

"You look lovely, my precious," Ogran said, and even without meeting his eyes, his words curdled her stomach in disgust. She took a place by her mother, latching onto her arm for support as she kept her gaze on the ground.

"Bring out the intruder," Enrick decreed.

Laela looked up with a start in time to see Garon, still in shackles, escorted onto the lawn by four guards. Thank Ares he looked none the worse for wear, so he hadn't been beaten. Their eyes met, locked, and she prayed he could see the love pouring from hers.

"This," Enrick began loudly enough for all to hear even though he directly addressed Ogran, "is the man I told you about. As Laela is to be your wife, it is fitting for you to choose how he dies."

Laela's heart plummeted and she feared she might be sick.

If Ogran took mercy, he might choose some quick method of death, a hanging, a beheading—gruesome but probably painless. Yet if he chose to punish Garon—and punish her, too—he might select something slow and torture-filled. Her heart threatened to explode through her chest at this horribly grim turn of events.

She did the only thing she could think to do—she broke free from her mother and threw herself at Ogran's feet. "Please, Ogran, make it a quick death. Grant me this wish and I will be a good and obedient wife to you in every way." It was the greatest, *hardest* thing she could promise. *Please let it be enough.*

Yet Ogran completely ignored her! He didn't even deign to look down, simply stepped around her as if she were a piece of debris strewn in the grass.

"What is your name, boy?" he asked. She looked up to see his gaze steeled on the man she loved.

"Garon," he said, eyes narrowed, expression cold.

To her surprise, the old man flinched. "What did you say?"

Her lover blinked. "My name is Garon. Why?"

The old man's face seemed to droop even further than his wrinkles allowed, his jaw dropping. "And your mother. Is she living?"

Garon looked understandably confused. "No, she is not. Why?"

"What was *her* name?"

"Her name was Maraena. Why do you ask me this?"

Ogran appeared nearly overcome with emotion—from what, Laela had no idea.

Everyone looked on him with the same sense of bewilderment—until he dropped to his knees and held out his arms. "My son!" he cried. "You are my son, boy!"

Garon's heart dropped to his stomach. His grandfather had never told him anything about his father, not even his name, and he'd never cared enough to ask. But all the pieces he knew about the man fit with *this* man.

This man…was his father.

Rage roared through him, propelling him to lunge, despite the chains that held him. He heard their harsh clanking rattle as the men who held him lost their grips. Women screamed, and Enrick's voice echoed from somewhere near, yelling, "Restrain him!" His muscles ached and his chest burned with wanting to rip Ogran limb from limb, and he'd almost reached the old man when his captors jerked him back, yanking at the chains from behind and forcing him to stand rigid, at attention.

Still, he let the venom spill from his eyes as he said, "You raped my mother, you ass!" Then he spit at him, even though too much distance lay between them now for it to matter.

Ogran's expression filled with guilty indignation. "I...I did no such thing."

"You raped her!" Garon yelled. "You raped her and cared nothing when she died delivering me!"

Ogran's wrinkles relaxed slightly as he looked to Enrick, trying to absolve himself. "She was...but a servant girl. Not...terribly bright."

Despite himself, Garon tore at his shackles once more at the insult to his mother. "*She was but a servant girl.* That makes it acceptable to rape her? To force her against her will?" He knew many men in Caralon put themselves above women in most ways—perhaps he'd been guilty of it himself, maybe even *very* guilty—but few condoned something so barbaric as rape. Garon swung his gaze to Enrick. "You would marry your daughter to a rapist? To man who thinks it's his right to take sex from a woman against her will?"

Ogran looked shamed, worried, and addressed Enrick again. "As I said, she was but a silly housemaid. I would never force my dear Laela." He stepped toward her then, cupping her cheek is his grizzled hand, and she shrank back, horror shining in her eyes.

Garon's heart clenched at her fear and loathing of the old man—and at the very idea that his *father* would be her husband. His father, the *rapist*. And he knew in that moment that *somehow* he would get free from these chains and this fortress before they killed him. *Somehow* he would break away and follow them. He would find her, save her. He *had* to. He simply had to save his princess.

Laela looked toward Enrick, her eyes filled with a desperation that tore at Garon's soul. "It's true, Father, what Garon is saying about him. I heard Ogran say…well, I heard him say he enjoyed being rough, that he intended to take my virginity by force. Right before I ran away."

Garon watched the ruler's eyes slowly change—from confusion…to worry…to the horror of believing her. "Why…didn't you tell me this, Daughter?" He reached out to take her hand.

Laela squeezed her father's large fist in hers and for the first time in a very, very long time, began to feel her faith in him return—just a little. "I…I didn't think you cared what happened to me anymore, so I…didn't waste my breath."

Oh, the warmth that flooded her when her father drew her into a crushing embrace. "Of course I care, Laela," he said above her, pressing her into his chest. "I cherish you. I simply…" He let out a long, tired sigh. "I let myself be blinded for a while," he admitted softly.

Within seconds, though, all softness fled his countenance as he released Laela from his embrace and scowled at Ogran. "Escort this man and his caravan from the fortress grounds. In fact, escort him well away from Myrtell, back to the mountains. Ogran, you are no longer welcome here!"

Ogran's eyes flashed dark with ire. "We had an arrangement, Enrick! You can't just change your mind. You promised the girl to me!"

"I can indeed change my mind, Ogran. I could banish you from all of Caralon, if I wish, so if I were you, I'd go peacefully and quickly before I do just that."

The old man's gaze narrowed. "What about the mountain passes? Who will protect them if I don't? This girl is all that stands between safety for all of Caralon and invasion. Wouldn't it be a pity if the Virgs discovered the path through the mountains? I know the passes well, and I'm not too old to start a war, my friend."

Enrick crossed his arms firmly across his chest, looking like the strong, admirable man Laela had always known her father to be. "I thought keeping Caralon secure and safe was more important to me than anything—but I realize now I was wrong. My family is more important. My *daughter* is more important. Do your worst, Ogran—we shall be ready."

All watched in silence as Ogran turned to go, his entourage trailing silently behind with a large number of Enrick's guards flanking them on either side. Laela's heart soared with liberation. The old man was gone! Out of her life, finally—no longer a threat to her! She closed her eyes and breathed a sigh of relief.

Just then, her father's hands gently gripped her

shoulders, turning her to face him. "Laela, my dear Laela," he said, his eyes looking heavy with emotion. "I thought I knew what was best for my daughters—and maybe, for Maven and Teesia, I did. But along the way I let other things get in the path of my good intentions. I grew foolish, and I forgot what was important. Will you forgive me, Laela?"

She swallowed back the lump in her throat—she'd never seen her father contrite and, given that he was Caralon's greatest warrior and the ruler of all, it took her aback. Yet she stood strong and tried not to let her more tender emotions show. "Are you still going to choose my husband?"

"Yes, Laela," he said softly but surely, "I am."

Her heart dropped, her hopes being dashed with her father's crushing words.

Until he added, "I choose this man," and pointed to Garon. "If he wishes it."

Laela looked to her lover, still in chains, his eyes filled with the ardor that had kept her heart beating through all the horrors of the past few days.

"It would be my great honor to be your husband, princess. If *you* wish."

"If *I* wish?" she repeated, a giddy giggle bubbling from her throat. She went to him, wrapping tight around him as his shackled arms closed about her waist. "Even during my Orientation, Garon, I wished it were *you* who would be my husband. And now, thank Ares, you *will* be! It is…a dream come true."

Without a care for who was watching, Laela lifted a long, hot kiss to Garon's warm mouth, letting herself descend into a familiar and sizzling passion, aware that her breasts ached for him and her pussy burned with need. She was fully lost to it for a long moment before the sound of her father clearing his throat reminded her they stood on the fortress lawn in front of a gathering of people.

Pulling back, she offered her father a sheepish look of apology, but his small smile said she need not be embarrassed.

As Garon's captors began to unchain him, Laela asked, "But what about the mountain passes, Father? What will we do?"

He shook his head slightly. "That's not for you to worry about any longer, Laela, and it never should have been. But I will speak with Dane about sending an army down into the mountains from Rawley to protect the passes, and I trust he will keep them covered until he, Ralen and I can put together a permanent plan for the region. And then...well, then we will commence with the Giving Ceremony and the wedding!"

ALL AROUND THE fortress, people bustled. Riders had been dispatched to send for Maven and Dane in the north and Teesia and Ralen in the south. Seamstresses set about making clothes for a wedding. And though the official Giving Ceremony would not take place just yet,

Enrick was so repentant that he decreed they should have a large feast now, tonight, to celebrate Laela's betrothal to the man she loved, so cooks ran here and there, heating fires, slicing vegetables, preparing meats—and runners were sent to Myrtell to invite Garon's friends, as well.

As far as Laela knew, her father was in his private chamber, meeting with his advisors and the leaders of his army in discussions about how to assist Dane in the task he would soon be assigned of protecting the mountain passes as well as the northern border. And her mother had headed off to Myrtell with the head seamstress to see Teesia's old friend, Bella, about designing a dress for Laela to be wed in.

All of which meant it seemed a safe time for the bride-to-be to drag her man off to her bedchamber.

Curling her hand around his wrist, she drew him inside and shut the door, then pressed him back against it with her body, making sure he felt each and every one of her curves. She ached for him like never before, and when he let out a short growl and lifted his hands to her breasts through the dress she wore, she moaned and knew her nipples had just perked to life beneath his hot touch.

Without delay, she smoothed her palm over his crotch, purring with pleasure when she felt the rock-hard column that had grown for her there. "Mmm, I want this, my master."

"And I'm going to give it to you, my little slave.

Hard." With that, he thrust his cock slightly against her hand and it seemed to reverberate all through her, right down into her cunt.

But just then, he flinched, his eyes shifting to something behind her. "What in Ares name…?"

She turned to see what had interrupted them and found him staring at Midnight, who lay in a tidy oval shape on the bed. "I told you about Midnight, remember? And he was here the other night when you came, too—but I guess you didn't see him then because it was dark. I do hope you like cats."

Garon's handsome face looked slightly bewildered for a moment, before his mouth twisted into a soft smile. "I still don't quite understand why someone would keep a cat indoors like he's a person, but…if it's a cat you want, princess, then it's a cat you shall have."

"Good. Because Midnight is my best friend."

He shifted her back into his arms and playfully lowered his chin. "Better than me?"

She grinned. "You shall both have to share my affections."

Her lover raised his eyebrows in wicked teasing. "I might share you with him when it comes to friendship, but that's where I draw the line. From now on, you're all mine, princess." With that, he moved toward the bed and shooed the cat from the fur covering. "Go away, Midnight. We need some privacy."

With a possessive look twinkling in his blue eyes, Garon pushed her softly to the bed, slid his knee between her legs, pressing his thigh against her lush pussy as his hard cock melded with her hip, then thrust aside the peach-colored silk at her breasts to free the mounds he longed to suckle.

Taking one ripe peak into his mouth, he listened to her moan, let the heated sound sink into his soul, let himself revel in the fresh knowledge that she was truly his now, forever, and that there was no longer anything to fear, nothing to stand in their way. "I love you, princess."

"I love you, too…master," she said with a naughty smile that drove his hand up beneath her dress, his fingers pressing immediately into the soft flesh of her cunt and inside.

"Oh…" she groaned at the gentle impact, and she was so wet and welcoming on his fingers that he couldn't go slow—he had to have more, now.

A moment later, he was parting her legs, thrusting his hot cock deep inside her warm, slick pussy, feeling her wrap around him, feeling that bond with her that would now never have to be broken.

"Fuck me, master," she whispered heatedly in his ear as he drove into her wetness, deep, deeper. "Yes, fuck me. Be my master. Make me obey."

Her words drove him onward, giving him immeasurable power, adding force to every stroke until he was pummeling her with them, making her cry out, reminding them both how much they'd come to love playing master and slave together.

It was without warning that Laela gripped his shoulders hard and pushed, turning him onto his back so that she could ride him. Her dress fell at her waist, her beautiful breasts bouncing as she rubbed herself against him, taking him so deep, hugging his cock tight—and when she came, her hot, lovely cries echoing off the stone walls to permeate his soul, he spilled himself inside her, coming just as hard, just as brutally, until they collapsed together in a tousled heap on the bed.

"You know," he said a long, satiated moment later, flashing an amused look, "when I first demanded you be my slave, it was supposed to scare you, princess."

She curled into his chest, her still-beaded nipples brushing lightly against his skin. "In the beginning, agreeing to be your sex slave *did* seem like a frightening sacrifice. But…turned out that it was no sacrifice at all."

EPILOGUE

THE HEM OF Laela's green dress blew around her legs in the sea breeze as she walked hand in hand with Garon over the sand to where her family stood with the priest waiting to join them in marriage.

She smiled at her eldest sister Maven, holding her baby daughter Kateene, who sported blonde hair just like her mother. Dane stood looking like his majestic warrior self, one hand poised lovingly at his wife's back.

Next came Teesia, her dark hair shining in the sun, her warm expression letting Laela feel how happy her sister was for her. Her equally dark, sensual husband, Ralen, stood in his usual black leather at her side, and to round out the group, Teesia held a basket wherein rested an obedient Midnight, who offered up a gentle meow as Laela approached.

To their right, Laela found Baelor, smiling on the joyous occasion, and her parents, both of whom she'd never seen look more pleased or content.

Now that a little time had passed, she'd almost forgiven her father—he'd spent the last two weeks telling her over and again how wrong he'd been, how his own power had blinded him, and she knew her happiness was truly important to him now. She'd also finally relayed to him the horrid behavior of his men upon capturing her, and he'd assured her he would punish them appropriately. Releasing Garon's hand, Laela went to her parents, giving them each a small hug and a kiss on the cheek.

When she turned back, she found Garon talking with the other men. "So," Dane said to him, "will you be joining us in defending Caralon for future generations?"

But her husband-to-be only laughed in the easy way she loved. "Enrick has kindly offered me a position, but I do well enough running the tavern. I built it on my own and I shall keep running it."

"Then it's down to us," Ralen said, a slight, challenging smile curving his lips as he glanced to Dane. "One of us will eventually rule Caralon."

"And the other?" Garon asked.

At this, both men looked to their wives, who now stood a few steps away cautiously introducing Kateene to Midnight.

Dane let out a content sigh. "Once upon a time, ruling Caralon was all that mattered to me. But now…well, either way, I am a happy man with a fuller life than I could have imagined."

"I, too, hope to rule this domain someday," Ralen said. "But if it doesn't come to pass, it simply means more time spent with Teesia, and only a foolish man would dare complain about such a bounty."

"Are we ready to begin?" the priest asked, and then began the traditional wedding ceremony, not the one of royal marriages as her other two sisters had experienced, but the vows spoken by those who *chose* to be joined.

"What gift have you for your bride?" the priest, a merry, plump older fellow asked Garon.

Garon's eyes sparkled as he presented Laela with a rolled sheet of parchment. She untied the ribbon that held it, opening it to find a charcoal sketch of a lovely stone home—certainly not the fortress in which she'd been raised, yet grander than most in Myrtell. She lifted her gaze to his.

"I plan to build you this home, Laela, on a stretch of land that lies halfway between your father's fort and the tavern, so that I can be close to my business while you will be close to your family. We can both have what we enjoy most—other than each other," he added with a wink. "And each room shall possess a viewing glass, for I know you have missed them."

As the gathering chuckled lightly at that, Laela smiled up at him, touched by the wonderful gesture of a splendid new home. "And there will be room for Midnight, of course?"

He laughed. "Of course. We wouldn't want the stable cat to sleep outside. Speaking of which, I also have this for you." Reaching into a pocket at the front of his pants, he extracted a bracelet, stretching it out for her to see—it featured a cat's face to match the pendant at her throat.

She gasped at the sight. "Oh Garon!"

"I had it commissioned from a jeweler in the village on the day you agreed to become my wife."

Carefully, he tied it about her wrist, and her body hummed with wanting him.

"And your gift for your groom?" the priest asked Laela.

Turning to her mother, she took the sack she'd asked Jalal to carry to the ceremony for her and she pulled out an ancient book from her father's library—one of her very favorites, which Enrick had agreed to part with at her request.

Upon seeing it, Garon exchanged a knowing look with her, and she knew he was pleased. He ran his hands over the aged cover of fraying threads, which in very faded words read *Fairy Tales*.

"These stories," she said to him, "all end just the way that our *new* story is beginning."

Returning her soft smile, Garon opened the book to the last page, running his fingers over the words printed on the fragile yellowed paper, and read the last sentence out loud.

"'As the king watched, the handsome young man kissed the beautiful princess, taking her as his bride. And they all lived happily ever after.'"

LOOK FOR MORE BOOKS FROM THE
BRIDES OF CARALON SERIES:

Rituals of Passion
Master of Desire

And don't miss any of these romantic erotica titles in print from Lacey Alexander:

Hot in the City
French Quarter
Sin City
Key West

H.O.T. Cops
Bad Girl By Night
Party of Three
Give in to Me

Other Print Titles
What She Needs
The Bikini Diaries
Seven Nights of Sin
Voyeur

And find out more about available Lacey Alexander titles,
including available ebook titles, at
www.laceyalexander.net

ABOUT THE AUTHOR

Lacey Alexander's books have been called deliciously decadent, unbelievably erotic, exceptionally arousing, blazingly sexual, and downright sinful. In each book, Lacey strives to take her readers on the ultimate erotic adventure and hopes her books will encourage women to embrace their sexual fantasies. Lacey resides in the Midwest, and when not penning romantic erotica, she enjoys history and traveling, often incorporating favorite travel destinations into her work.

Learn more about Lacey and her books at www.laceyalexander.net, or sign up for her newsletter and follow her on Facebook to get all the latest news and have a chance to win signed books and other prizes.